MISS AGNÈS

THE AGNÈS DUET #1

HANNAH BYRON

Editor: Poppet
Cover Design: Poppet
More info: hannahbyron.com
ISBN eBook:978-90-830892-7-0
ISBN Paperback: 978-90-830892-2-5

"Stop acting so small.
You are the universe in ecstatic motion."

~ Rumi ~

AUTHOR'S NOTE

The Edwardian novella *Miss Agnès* was originally published in 2016 with the title *The Blood Red Nails of War* as part of an Anthology with other authors

I wrote *Miss Agnès* and its sequel *Doctor Agnès* as finger exercises for my *Resistance Girl Series*. They are only loosely related to the first book in that series, *In Picardy's Fields*, so if you've read that book, you'll find *The Agnès Duet* differs substantially.

Miss Agnès paints the prewar years of the French-Swedish Agnès Baroness Gunarsson de Melancourt and her rough-and-tumble with the freethinking inhabitants of Château de Dragancourt in Picardy: Elle and Jacques.

Doctor Agnès is about the young doctor's return to Château de Dragancourt in 1917. The castle has been transformed into a frontline hospital, but the same inhabitants are in charge. Can they come to terms with their past fallout in the middle of war?

I hope you will enjoy these rewritten novellas.

1

MISS AGNÈS

Château de Melancourt, Picardy, July 1908

For now, all was peace and perfection at Château de Melancourt, the robust medieval fortress lying amid Picardy's rolling hills. For now.

The stronghold of Agnès's youth was at a good day's drive from Paris, and as such only used as a summer residence by the Baron Dupuis de Melancourt and his adoptive daughter.

Summer offered them a welcome season of repose and recuperation from the long winter months in the French capital. Both the Baron, a widowed musician with an inclination to introversion, and his teenage daughter, Agnès, treasured the time away from the busy schedule of social obligations that the Baron's position entailed.

There was nothing Agnès Gunarsson de Melancourt liked more than to read in the shade of the old chestnut tree in the castle's garden. Once she'd done some pages of reading she would stare out over the mown lawn, savoring the beauty of the prose, her slender, pale hand cupping her chin.

A fountain gurgled at the center of the lawn, water spewing from a jumping fish's mouth while bumble bees hummed about the Buddleia bushes.

At her feet, as always, lay Gåva, the sheepdog she and her father had brought home from Sweden fifteen years earlier. Gåva, her black and tan coat motley and matted now, was blind, and almost deaf, but her gray-haired nose made up for her other declining senses.

Even the slightest movement of Miss Agnès's legs was registered by the loyal dog, and she guarded her mistress as she had once done Ingrid, the young lady's mother.

Wherever Agnès sat down Gåva laid as a foothold. She even slept in a wicker basket beside Agnès's bed, much to the disapproval of her father, Max, who had always tolerated and respected this remnant of his daughter's unfortunate past, but in essence viewed the animal as a mere carrier of lice.

"Dearest," he tried every time, "You simply cannot take Gåva to Madame Guilliard's tea party, or to the Duke of Bourbon's ball."

But it all fell on deaf ears. As pliant as Agnès was in all other matters her dog was her one living memory of the country of her birth. So she wouldn't part with her, like a young child would hang on to its toy tiger.

Knowing of the girl's obsessive devotion to her dog Max feared the moment the two of them would have to part, to the extent that it kept him awake at night, wondering whether he should introduce a new playmate to his daughter or take her on an extended vacation when the sad time of Gåva's passing arrived.

As if aware that she had been the subject of such heavy considerations, the dog lifted her old head and nuzzled her nose in Agnès's long skirts. Stroking the head absentmindedly, her mistress read to her,

"I don't quite see," she answered, "where in particular it strikes you that my danger lies. I'm not conscious, I assure you, of the least 'disposition' to throw myself anywhere. I feel as if, for the present, I have been sufficiently thrown."

Gåva put her head down again, satisfied with her mistress's contentment with her reading. There was no need for action here. She was soon fast asleep, lips quivering every time she exhaled.

Agnès, with a thinking wrinkle in her smooth forehead, pondered what Henry James might be meaning with this early foreboding.

She had just begun reading *The Wings of The Dove*, and was still acquainting herself with the unfortunate Kate Croy's fate. As always Agnès compared the lives of her fictitious heroines to her own life. There was nothing she feared right now.

All that had been hard and difficult was in the past, in that northern European country where winter nights lasted all day and summer days had no end. A country she simultaneously loved and loathed; because it had been Mama's country, but it had taken her too.

As every other day in that summer of 1908, Agnès was blissfully happy under her chestnut tree in the château's afternoon garden. She lacked nothing.

Through the open window she could hear her father practice Theodore Moses-Tobani's *Hearts and Flowers*. He'd explained he was to play that partiture with his orchestra, *L'Esprit Musique,* at a garden party the following day. She was expected to join them.

"I don't particularly like us to break up our tranquil life here and go on a social call to strangers," Agnès mused, as she had often done since her father had announced the party. Every time she felt guilty over her egocentricity; for hadn't Papa taught her to put the demands of society before her own?

She knew he, himself, was not keen on leaving Melancourt to travel across Picardy in this heat. Ruminating she could hear his familiar tone.

"My dear child, it's a one-time invitation. The only one I've accepted all summer, so I think we have to put our best foot forward and simply let ourselves be entertained. Remember, I told you there are children your age there?"

Children her age. The idea was nice, Agnès had to admit, but she was generally quite satisfied to just have her two friends.

One was Katell, who lived across from her at the Plâce de Châtelet in Paris, and the other was Victor, her cousin. The son of Max's sister Bernadette, who stayed with them during his holidays from *Maison d'Éducation de la Légion d'Honneur* at Saint-Denis. Both Katell and Victor were more than enough for the bookworm, Agnès. And Gåva, of course, her very best friend.

Shards of her father's music floated into the garden. It sounded quite melancholic, but also very pure and ethereal.

Music was her father's passion, as books were hers. He devoted entire days to music; composing, teaching, and often performing as well. On many occasions he had tried to also get her enthusiastic about his métier, but Agnès sadly had no talent for music, not even for singing. Unlike her mother apparently, whose beautiful soprano her father often spoke about with a soft rasp in his voice.

The Baron had not easily surrendered his attempts to teach his daughter music; first they had tried the piano, then the violin, even several wind instruments, but Agnès couldn't even master reading notes and continued to sing horribly off key.

"You stick with your books and I'll do the music for you," Papa had finally exclaimed after the last failed attempt. But there were no hard feelings, he just wanted her to be happy. It was not only books that were Agnès's passion, but also writing, and at fifteen years of age had announced that she wanted to study Languages and Philosophy at the Sorbonne when she turned eighteen.

The latest craze she had discovered was the American author Henry James, whose every novel she devoured with a speed that hardly kept the book deliveries arriving in time.

Home-tutored, Agnès was well-versed in French, English, Swedish and Latin, and also spoke a substantial mouthful of German and Spanish. She preferred to only read fiction in French and English.

'My little scholar' her father dotingly called her. So her future was clear to all.

Gåva had become accustomed to her mistress exclaiming dramatic parts of her much-loved novels aloud, and although Swedish to the bone, the old dog, like no other, understood the love for words in any expressible human language.

Life was good, really good. "Finally," Papa would say, "our ship is sailing through calm waters."

Agnès did not look French at all. In fact there could not be a bigger difference outwardly between the dark-haired, olive-skinned baron, and the very blonde, blue-eyed nymph from the north. They were complete opposites, no matter how alike they were inwardly; both even-tempered, sensitive, and artistic.

Agnès always held herself in a distinct yet modest and upright way. A quiet person, who thought deeply and discerned everything. Those who had known her mother, the unfortunate vicar's daughter Ingrid Gunarsson of the island in the Baltic Sea, would have seen a striking likeness between mother and daughter but only on the outside. Her mother, Ingrid was told, was all vivacity and spirit.

The Baron, sadly, wasn't Agnès's real father, but he told her he'd loved her deceased mother so very much, and for that reason alone felt Agnès to be his daughter in every possible way but the biological.

"I could not have a better Papa in the whole world," she told him every night before tiptoeing upstairs in her nightdress, being tucked in by the old housekeeper, Madame Proulx.

"And I could not have prayed for a better daughter," was Papa's daily retort.

Papa and Agnès were cheek by jowl so no one ever doubted her pedigree, despite their complete contrast in exterior appearance.

Agnès's real father was a man whose history was shrouded in mystery. Papa Max had told her his name was Kalle Ljundberg and that he was probably somewhere in the United States of America. A Swede by birth he had left her mother unwed – hence Agnès's surname being a combination of her mother's last name and her father's titled name.

When Agnès turned sixteen on the 4th of April 1909, Papa Max had promised to tell the apple of his eye everything about the vague circumstances of her birth and the relationship of her parents. Until that age, he had felt her to be too young and impressionable to deal with her difficult start in life.

But whenever Agnès pressed him with questions about her mother, Papa Max was all too willing to answer them outright.

"Do tell me about when you were Mamas tutor," was enough to get his eyes shining and embarking on an anecdote of one of her mother's pranks as a girl about Agnès's age, which would make them both smile through their tears.

Agnès particularly liked the story where Ingrid was promised a ball for her 16th birthday by her father, the Vicar, and couldn't concentrate on her lessons because of her excitement.

"She would run to the window every time with the excuse that she heard something being brought for her, or the arrival of her beloved brother Johan. The only way I could make her concentrate on her lessons was by letting her play the piano and sing. That was your mother's real passion. *Peer Gynt Suite*, in particular was her absolute favorite, and I could let her sing *Solveig's Song* whenever she was distracted. You know she was singing that to you when I finally found the two of you in that godforsaken ruin?"

And thus the story would always return to her mother's misfortune and how Papa had rescued them both, but Mama had already been too weak when the rescuers finally came.

The most poignant reminder of her mother was a framed photograph of the young Ingrid Gunarsson which stood on the grand piano in the music room.

She was dressed in a beautiful but quite outmoded dress, embroidered with tiny white roses; soft-looking material with lace lining. Her light hair was also styled in an old-fashioned way, all heaviness at the front in thick rolls of springy light hair, making her look too old for her young age.

The eyes were striking, and although it was a black and white photograph the clear light in them sprang at anyone who looked; there was zest for life and mockery in equal doses in the gaze and the mouth, with soft full lips, smiling bountifully, showing two rows of perfect, strong teeth.

The photograph had become full of color for young Agnès, because Papa Max had ordered the French symbolist painter Edgar Maxence to paint a portrait of the photo, and this large painting was hanging over the mantelpiece in the same music room. The two reproductions had melted into one in Agnès's vision, and as they were the only visual image she had of her mother she looked at them every day, sometimes several times.

Though she had no real memory of her, Papa made sure her mother remained as present in her life as she could. Every year, at the end of winter, they undertook the travel of more than twelve hundred miles from Paris to the graveyard in Smedby village, on the island of Öland. Just to pay their respects and clean the tomb.

Ingrid had been buried in a remote spot in the same graveyard where Agnès's grandparents, Elisabet Gunarsson-Holm and Gustav Gunarsson, lay side-by-side. They would also quickly pass by their tomb, but Agnès didn't like the concerned frown on her father's forehead when they did.

It was a solemn journey, but her father doggedly held on to it and Bertrand, Papa's chauffeur, steered them safely across all of Europe without so much as a frown or complaint.

"Agnès, where are you?" her father's clear melodious voice sounded from the open window.

"*Ici*, Papa." She threw the book down in her chair and dashed towards the house. Gåva followed as quickly as her old legs would carry her.

Tea-time was quality time, the two of them together.

2

MADEMOISELLE ELLE

Château de Dragancourt, Picardy, July 1908

I t was another monotonous summer day in the French countryside. Life had slid into sleepy laziness, where time seemed of no consequence and everything was lacquered over with a haze of placidness. Even the dragonflies seemed to hang in midair, their wings motionless, undecided in which direction to take off next. *Where was the buzz of Paris, when one needed it?*

Elle de Dragancourt was trailing her hand through the water of the pond, luring the fat koi towards her with her blood-red fingernails. When they were about to bite she would quickly withdraw her hand. The Parisienne waited for the red-and-white fish to give up their hunt for food and swim away before she would dip her fingers back in, wetting her Valencienne lace cuffs without care.

Boredom had set in with Elle due to the long summer days, the lack of company, and the quietude of country life, but none of her brethren seemed to care the least bit for how depressed she felt.

Nothing went her way these days. Not since '*la petite affaire*' that had made her blood sing and her father cringe.

"Phah!" Elle told the fish, "I haven't seen Daniel Westport for ages, so Papa could give me some respite! And here's him thinking I broke it off because of his *I-forbid-you* sermon. I'm not in the least bit interested in Daniel Westport, nor in his boss André de Tremoille. After you've seen one man, you've seen them all. Men are so boringly predictable."

The tall girl, with her willowy figure and shiny black hair around a pale narrow face, abandoned her idling at the side of the pond and got up, stretching her long legs and adjusting her blue-silk afternoon dress. Even talking to herself was no fun at all. Where was there still some fun to be had?

Her two younger sisters, Marie-Antoinette and Madeleine, could be heard playing a game of tennis in the court at the back of the family's country estate. Her twin brother, Jacques, was lounging under a parasol on the lawn, immersed in Henry James's *The Wings Of The Dove,* his flanneled legs draped dandishly over the side of his lounge seat.

Her siblings always seemed to adapt more easily to this languid summer style of living, whereas Elle yearned for the Paris boulevards, for gossiping with her girl-friends, Bonny and T-Rose, in Les Tuileries, and for racing around de Arc de Triomphe twelve times in her father's Ford T.

~

AS THEY DID EVERY YEAR, and thus also this July in 1908, Count Horace de Dragancourt and his English wife Virginia had left their stately mansion on the Boulevard Hauptmann in Paris for Château de Dragancourt in the *Departement Roye,* to spend the summer months away from the city. Aside from their four children, aged ten to eighteen, they always brought along their cook, the two kitchen maids, Dolly and Daisy, Virginia's private maid, and Guillaume, the chauffeur who also doubled as the butler.

Local staff was hired for the rest of the work, and then there were the gardeners for the garden *à la Française,* and the stable boys for the Arabian horses the Dragancourt girls were fond of riding.

~

LISTLESS, Elle sauntered over to where her brother hung in his chair, and seeing he had dozed off with his book half in his lap she pinched his dangling calf with the edges of her sharp nails.

Jacques woke with a start. "Ouch, hell, I've been stung by a wasp!"

First he gazed at his pantaloon in annoyance, then started hitting it to get rid of the unseen insect.

"Something like it, you lazy bum."

Snickering, Elle turned her back on him to continue her leisurely stroll to the tennis court to see what her sisters were up to.

Just then she heard the tires of a vehicle crunch the

gravel in the drive. A car door slammed. Only one. She changed course.

That must be De Trémoille arriving, perhaps Daniel had accompanied him. Adopting a mock angelic expression on her pretty face, Elle made her way around the side of the castle to welcome their first guest of the day.

Alexandre, tall, elegant, and middle-aged, towered over her as he took her hand to kiss it, ignoring the traces of waterweed his lips had to brush.

His gray-green gaze didn't leave her dark one, but Elle withdrew her hand and snapped,

"Where's Daniel? I thought you'd bring him with you?"

"Hello to you too, mademoiselle Elle. What a nice surprise to see you again!"

La Trémoille, well aware he was considered a 'mere' businessman, although rich beyond means but not of blue blood, sounded irritated by the young girl's haughty tone. Especially as he knew – like *tout Paris* – how de Count's daughter had lowered herself only weeks earlier with Daniel Westport, his New-York business associate, and a man maybe twenty years younger but of much lower esteem even than he.

"Oh, sorry old chap, yes, hello to you too!" Elle shrugged at his hostile approach and immediately looked for ways to get away from him now she knew he hadn't brought Daniel.

"I thought your father didn't approve of your liaison with Westport?" He raised an eyebrow. Just at that moment Elle's mother, the eternally gracious Countess Virginia de Dragancourt – whom everyone called Ginny – came flowing towards them, all perfume and *crêpe de mousseline.* A fairy-tale picture but the body underneath all that delicate elegance had a rigid and alabaster appearance as if she was the statue of the Venus of Milo herself. Her eyes, topaz like Elle's, had an icy gloss. Alexandre bent his bronzed head over the Countess's gloved hand and brushed the scented leather with his lips.

Ginny ignored her daughter and immediately locked arms with Alexandre, sending him a radiant smile from perfectly painted lips.

She announced in her high-pitched voice, *"Viens avec moi, dahling,* champagne is ready!" Only then did she turn her dark, well coifed head to Elle, and with a triumphant squint in her almond-shaped eyes, said, "Are you joining us on the terrace, honey?"

"No thank you, Mother, I'll let you oldies have fun together."

"Dinner at eight in *la grande salle verte,"* Ginny ordered, drifting lightly up the steps that led to the entrance of the castle, and disappearing inside.

Elle could hear her giggle resonate from the walls and a cold feeling raced up her veins.

"Damn them all!" She balled her fists.

For a moment she lingered outside on the gravel not knowing why the little scene with her mother and De Trémoille had unsettled her, and not knowing what to do next. Then she turned her attention to Alexandre's shiny white 120 HP Benz that stood pontifically on the driveway, still making clicking noises while cooling down from its sudden halt.

Elle sniffed around the long chassis of the 4-cylinder marvel with the striking black tires, so elegantly contrasting with the white body, like a dog in heat.

She simply had to hop in to feel the touch of the black leather upholstery, warmed by the sun and Alexandre's derriere. Gripping the copper wheel, so slender and round between her two hands; it felt swell, just swell.

This Benz had only three weeks earlier entered in the 1908 French Grand Prix in Dieppe, where it came in second. Boy was that something! How she would have loved to compete in that race, but it was only open to male drivers. Elle sniffed again, now with contempt.

"Ha! Women couldn't drive!" She knew better than that.

Compared to Jacques she was an absolute champion at the wheel. Her brother, oddly enough didn't even care for cars. All he cared for was cricket and rowing. He'd become a complete Oxford mold since he'd studied in England. No fun to be around anymore. Not like the old days of silly pranks and secret outings.

~

LIKE EVERY RICH and self-respecting aristocrat Count Horace de Dragancourt owned a motor vehicle, but in Elle's eyes it hardly deserved the label of car. It was an ugly black Ford model T that looked like a silly boy's toy compared to this racer.

Papa's car, which was considered just a motoring convenience, had never struck a chord in his high-strung daughter. Elle craved beauty in everything her eyes wandered over, and when that wandering eye rested on something of her liking, she simply had to have it.

Having a bone to pick with De Trémoille, as it was this insidious toad who'd given her father the hint about her affair with Daniel Westport, Elle's mind was made up. She was going to give the Benz a good ride. Pedal to the metal.

"It's just you and me now, beauty," she declared as she slid out of the seat to get a hold of the crank at front.

It was much harder to turn than she had anticipated, but after a couple of yanks the motor started unwillingly and Elle ran back to the driver's seat.

What now? She pushed a number of pedals and inspected the dials on the dashboard. The beauty squeaked quite shrilly, ending her protest in a grunting noise, then fell still. Elle spied around her to see if anybody was alerted to her activities by the noise, but the family was in the back garden behind the solid walls of the castle, so she decided to give it another go.

This time she struck the right pedal, obviously having released the hand-brake, and off she went, first making a semi-circle over the gravel in front, and then down the lane in between the old trees until she came to the Avenue de Paris.

The soft summer breeze undid Elle's hairdo, and long black strands whirled in her face and around the steering wheel, but she didn't give a damn.

"This is it!" she shouted to the wind, her mouth covetous and her topaz eyes reflecting the brilliance of exuberant youth.

People stopped at the side of the road; peasants returning home for their supper with bundles of straw or potatoes on their back, and a cyclist saved his own skin by hastily retiring to the strip of grass next to the tarmac when Elle almost knocked him over.

At first she swayed from left to right and back, it being fortunate that there was hardly any other traffic, but soon she got the hang of it and positioned herself strongly on the right side of the road.

Turning at Le Roi du Matelas, she stepped on the gas on the way back, reaching a top speed of eighty miles per hour. It was beyond exhilarating. It was the best thing she'd ever done in her life.

There and then Elle knew what she wanted to do; who she was going to be. Elle de Dragancourt was going to be the first French female race car driver ever. And she would have a car especially designed for her. Something like this Benz, but maybe even more glorious, but a Benz would otherwise have to do.

~

FOR THE FIRST time in days Elle was happy, she lacked nothing. Her soul was fulfilled. But it didn't last long. When she parked the car back in the courtyard and slowly made her way back to the castle, the longing started again.

Wanting a car like this, plans brewing inside of her to reach that dream, obstacles on that path to enter the world of car racers as a woman. The indifference about her lot, and always the fight to get attention, to be heard, to be taken seriously. The sulky expression on her face returned.

"But at least I have a dream now," she pepped herself up, "Maybe Daddy will listen this time. I just *have to* make him see that this is what I want. I have to find a way."

None of the family had noticed her disappearance. When she came down for cocktails, for once Elle looked quite subdued and just lovely in her lavender evening dress, low enough to show her modest bosom but high enough not to upset the Count.

Her mind was made up, so she had to lay low. Smiling sweetly, she feigned interest in the garden party that was to be held the next day, all the while planning and plotting on how to convince her father to back her new-found destiny.

"Cars are much more thrilling than men," Elle mused, sipping her Cuba Libre and keeping De Trémoille in her topaz gaze. "Cars are so twentieth century, whereas men are still stuck in the last epoch."

3

THE BARON

B aron Max came downstairs and stood on the carpet in the hall, smiling broadly at his protégé. Despite being of substantial means, the Baron always dressed casually and cared very little for protocol and decorum. He was in his early forties now, his dark hair only here and there with a silvery thread, his olive-skin a remembrance of his Spanish mother; a soft warm glow in his deep-brown eyes.

Max wasn't a remarkably handsome man, nor very imposing as he was not tall enough for that, but there was something in his posture, a mixture of tenacious morality and artistic kindness that made sure one didn't overlook Baron Maximilian Dupuis de Melancourt.

Today he wore embroidered Persian *babouches*, simple gray flannel trousers with a clear fold in them, and a rather wide navy cotton pullover under which the collar of his white chemise, with the invariably silk cravat tucked in, were visible.

He opened his arms wide and the blonde girl rushed

into her adoptive father's arms as if she were still five
years old. After the long cuddle as if they hadn't seen
each other at lunchtime, Max dutifully caressed the gray
head of the wildly tail-wagging Gåva before turning his
full interest to his daughter once more. "What were you
doing out there, *chérie*? The obvious?"

"Of course, Papa, have you ever read Henry James? I
think him extraordinary. Oh, if I only could compose
sentences like that."

"Henry James? No I haven't, my darling. Literature-
wise, I am quite a philistine at times. Do instruct me,
which of his books should I tackle first?"

"Start with *The Portrait of A Lady*, Papa. You'll like it,
it's quite artistic, like you."

This made the baron smile. Arm-in-arm they went
through the maze of corridors of the Château until they
came to the tearoom in the left wing, which also served as
a conservatory for Max's collection of oriental plants.

As it was a warm and sunny day the glass doors to the
garden were open and Justine, the maid, was busy setting
up their afternoon tea. Father and daughter enjoyed the
strong English brew with milk and sugar, accompanied
with a slice of fruitcake and a macaron.

The Baron wasn't frugal or sparing, but ever since he
had seen the extreme poverty in which his beloved Ingrid
had had to survive, he believed in not eating too much
between meals and loathed every form of frippery and
extravagance.

No room in Château de Melancourt was considered a
real room when it didn't have music, so even in the
conservatory there was a gramophone with a collection
of records. For this afternoon *O Sole Mio* sounded from

the big horn, a little scratchy at times but ever so soulful and theatrical.

"Tell me about De Dragoncourts," Agnès asked her father, as they were seated with their cups of tea and a macaron on their saucers. "After all, we're going to visit them tomorrow and I have no idea who they are."

The Baron, who had been giving his full attention to *O Sole Mio,* although he'd heard the piece at least a hundred times, scooted over to the gramophone to pick up the needle, after which the music abruptly stopped.

"Of course, my dear! I understand this afternoon party is a little foreign to you, but I truly thought you'd enjoy some young company. Didn't you meet Elle and Jacques last winter at Madame Guilliard's matinée? I'm quite sure you did."

The Baron frowned, trying to remember whether he had actually introduced the Dragancourt children to his daughter.

Agnès shook her head.

"I'd have remembered, Papa. I'm much better at remembering names and faces than you are. I'm positive we were never formally introduced. So is the Count a good friend of yours?"

The Baron wiped a small piece of pink macaron from his pantaloon.

"In a sense he is. I've known Horace forever. He's the typical diplomat, you know, all politics and old boys' networks. He's a good chap, though. We frequent the same clubs, bump into each other regularly. I don't know his wife very well. She's British, old aristocratic family but I've forgotten her maiden name. She's quite a boisterous and libertine lady, if you ask me."

"And what about the children?" Agnès implored further. Though her father looked on displeased, she meanwhile lifted Gåva onto her lap and when the dog had settled, started caressing the velvety ears.

"I'm afraid I know little more than the names, and vaguely their ages," the Baron observed. "The twins, Elle and Jacques, must be eighteen or nineteen, and then there are two younger girls, whose names and ages escaped me. You see, when the count and myself meet we seldom discuss our children, so I'm not well prepared to provide you with more detailed information."

"It's okay, Papa. It's a one-time thing going over to Dragancourt. If we don't enjoy it, we don't have to invite them back here, do we?"

The baron chuckled, lighting one of his thin Le Roy cigars and inhaling lightly.

"Why wouldn't we enjoy it, darling? Heavens, we can be terrible, can't we? Tucked away in our hiding place here in the country. I would never dream of not returning an invitation when in Paris."

"You always say different rules apply during the summer, Papa. But why did you never ask the Dragancourts over to Place de Châtelet?"

"I guess we're not on that level of familiarity. This invitation for a musical performance, during their tea party, came through our cellist. Patrick's apparently a good friend of the Countess. That's how it all came about."

"Tell me about their castle. Is it also a medieval fortress? You *have* been there?"

"Yes, I've been there once. That's one of the reasons for accepting the invitation. I simply want to show you the splendor of the place. Any visitor to Picardy should see the Château de Dragancourt. It's a pearl of classic French Renaissance architecture. Similar to the castles on Loire River, I'd say, a small version of the Château d'Amboise that we visited last year. Dragancourt bathes in history. The family is even older than ours."

The Baron took a pull on his cigar and winked at her. Agnès knew her father liked to mock the old French aristocracy who always puffed out their breasts about famous pedigree, and going back to Charlemagne or beyond.

"I'm sure I much prefer our drafty old-fashioned medieval vestige," Agnès joked back.

It was true that there was much that needed repair at Château de Melancourt but the baron could not bring himself to introduce all the novelties, like central heating and new plumbing.

"In summers we camp out," he always proclaimed and Agnès didn't care. Melancourt served its purpose for them.

The open fires in the rooms they used were always warm on chilly mornings and cold evenings. The maids always ensured there was enough hot water in her room and the toilet flushed.

True, she could not call her friend Katell on the telephone, but the girls wrote each other lengthy letters, and every arrival of a new scented envelope was the highlight of Agnès's day.

"Well, tell me, Papa, about this important Dragancourt history. It might help me see Elle and Jacques in the light of their old and famous bloodline."

She knew her father liked history like nothing else,

and couldn't wait to lecture her on all the ins and outs of this grand castle she was about to lay eyes on.

"Are you sure?" The Baron scanned her face. "Let's have fresh tea first and then I'll bore you a little longer." He pulled the bell cord and the maid peeked her head around the conservatory door.

"More tea and more of your delicious macarons, Justine." The Baron waved his elegant arms in a gesture of great approval. The maid smiled, happy with the compliment. "Ready for the insight?" he asked Agnès.

She nodded.

"Dragancourt derives its name from the coat of arms of Louis, first Count of Dragancourt, who had the castle built in the 16th century by the famous architect Philibert Delorme. The count could have chosen an Italian designer, of course, which was very much *en vogue* at the time, and that's why it's silly that we call it *French* classic Renaissance architecture as most of the castles were designed by Italians like Leonardo da Vinci, but never mind that. Apparently Louis knew Delorme personally. Well, their cooperation led to a château of great refinement and elegance, which makes even my French heart beat a little more chauvinistically."

Agnès laughed out loud. Though her father was on numerous committees involving state affairs, often grudgingly, because he was close friends with Prime Minister Georges Clemenceau, he was always reprimanded by his peers for being too un-French.

"What's there to laugh at?" The Baron smirked. "Well, anyway, our good friend Louis, the first Count of Dragancourt, was a member of the Bourbon family and a leader of the Protestant party. That's why he'd chosen the sign of the dragon in combination with the French court for his coat of arms. The Dragancourt castle became one of the strongholds of the religious wars that pestered France in the 16th century. That's why it has two impressive gatehouses, and an underground jail with an intricate locking system."

"Gosh," Agnès exclaimed. "Do we have something similar, here, Papa?"

"I'm afraid not, my pet. I think my ancestors were as apolitical as I am. Must run in our veins. As far as I can trace my roots we're a line of poets, musicians, with the odd philosopher and writer thrown in. No storming the barricades or heroic battle facts on behalf of the Melancourts. Ah well, there's a place for everyone in God's eyes."

Agnès studied her adoptive father, his musical elegance and slim figure, and could not picture him holding a banner while shouting "*Vive la Révolution.*"

The Baron put one flanneled leg over the other and continued with his discourse.

"During the 18th century when the Sun King reigned, the castle became a showpiece for the arts and music. You'll understand that's the period I studied most about it."

The Baron gave her a happy smile, which Agnès returned. Anything artistic made her father's blood sing.

He continued, "We had by then landed at the sixth generation of Dragancourts, and this specific specimen was named Philippe. Though the Dragancourts had always been rich aristocrats, Philippe managed to become exorbitantly rich, not because of his many talents but through his choice of marriage partner. He managed to secure the hand of the daughter of the Marquis de la Raye, who was known for his lucrative trading in the Indies.

Much of the castle's final frippery was due to Philippe. He brought the Italian atmosphere of the famous architect Servandoni, and apparently parties held at Dragancourt were almost the equivalent of the Versailles balls. With much of the same decadence and excess we know about these carnivalesque events. Well, I haven't witnessed them with my own eyes, of course, but that's what the research tells." The Baron chuckled again.

"Gosh," was all Agnès repeated.

"The current 9th Count de Dragancourt, Horace, lives comfortably on the wealth gathered by his predecessors," her father added. "I'm told he has little interest, or insight, in changing so much as one painting in the Oudry wing, or a mirror in the Servandoni ballroom, or a shaped box tree in the nine acre park. But Horace loves all the newest devices: electrical light, telephone, central heating."

Max looked at her almost apologetically, knowing how Agnès missed their Paris telephone, but she ignored it.

"So Papa, do you gather, the family is still a little wild and exorbitant today?"

"Who knows? The count isn't, as far as I can tell. But it's hard to close your ears to the Paris gossip about the Countess, even if you try to. Well, we'll see about all that tomorrow. I hope the children are nice."

Agnès wanted to ask what was so notorious about the Countess de Dragancourt, but knew her father didn't approve of gossip, so bit her tongue. It would be a nice thing to find out together with Katell, when they met again in the fall.

Father and daughter finished their tea in perfect harmony, with Gåva snoring softly in Agnès's lap. Their afternoon in the cozy conservatory, of the far from exorbitant Melancourt castle, lacked very little. But would it last?

4

THE PREPARATIONS

T he morning of the tea party was passing in an absolute frenzy at Château de Dragancourt. Expected were only some thirty guests, but of very different plumage, and it proved rather complex to organize it in such a way that the differing tastes of the callers would not clash but would result in a highly talked-about harmonious and musical affair.

There would be foreign diplomats with their mistresses, and young Impressionistic artists with their own quirks and needs, young children and old matrons. Far from a homogenous group.

"For sure, Horace!" Ginny exclaimed in her upper-class British voice, red-tipped nails demonstratively on her slender hips. "How can you expect me to do honor to the Dragoncourt *famille* out of season, when our children are running wild and the hired staff is altogether unreliable?"

"You'll pull it off as always, Gin-Gin." The Count shrugged, while he continued to read his morning paper, rolling the tips of his impressive mustache between thumb and forefinger. "I thought we'd decided on this party so the children would run less wild and the staff would learn how to behave. I'm personally really looking forward to the performance of Baron Max and his quartet. You know their cellist, Patrick Berlioz, don't you, *chérie*?"

"Oh him," the Countess raised her shoulders inside the aqua cardigan in a disinterested way. "Paddy's okay. I don't expect him to misbehave."

"Well, what's the problem then, my dear? I honestly believe you should stop fussing over it and leave it all in the hands of the staff. What am I paying them for so lavishly, if they can't do their jobs? Now, let me read my paper and only interrupt me in case of a real calamity?" His grizzled head had already disappeared inside *Le Matin*.

Countess Virginia, wearing an elegant morning dress of white silk with the draped cardigan and high-heeled sandals, stood for a moment staring at the newspaper with a frown between her smoky eyes.

She wanted to say: *"You know I hate giving orders about practical matters, especially when we're understaffed and the maids are constantly fighting with one another, but what would you care about that, husband?"* But she stayed silent and made her way to the kitchen to see if the Château was not yet on fire.

The two kitchen maids, Daphne and Dolly, who on normal days didn't get on very well as Daphne, born and bred in Paris, considered herself a liege above provincial Dolly, but then Dolly was prettier than coarsely-built Daphne, so the squabble never ended.

"I saw your beau show interest in you alright, yesterday at the village pump," Virginia heard Daphne snap at Dolly, who was making the pastry for the apple pies.

"No 'e didn't!" Dolly shouted back in her unpolished accent. "I 'ave no interest in your Jean-Batiste. You know I 'ave a beau of me own back 'ome."

Jean-Batiste was one the family's gardeners.

"I saw him clack his tongue at you and you must have wriggled your hips to make him do that. You're always trying to get what I have."

"No, I'm not. You're a liar." Dolly threw a handful of flour in Daphne's direction. It covered half of her face, her apron, and the front of her dress. Daphne howled and flung herself at Dolly, tearing at the dark locks that peeped from under her bonnet.

"Stop it!" Virginia shrieked, and the two girls, Daphne covered in white powder and with a fistful of Dolly's hair, and Dolly's clasping her head in pain, stared at the white ghost of their mistress, frozen in their places.

"What is all this nonsense about a beau when you have dozens of things to do?" the Countess chastised shrilly, but then sank onto a kitchen chair and started to moan.

Now they would certainly never pull it off to have all the delicacies for the tea party ready in time. It was utterly impossible to steer this staff in any particular direction.

"Sorry, Milady." Two subdued maids looked around the kitchen where the chaos was now complete, and then at their distressed mistress who usually was all disinterested calm.

"You're simply not up to the task." Virginia sniffed. "Fetch the Count. Now!"

~

BY MID-MORNING, realizing the state of affairs was spiraling towards *catastrophe*, the Count ordered Guillaume, the chauffeur annex butler, to drive to *Boulangerie Patrice* in the center of Roye to buy the cakes and pastries required for the party, while the two girls get the flour out of their hair and calmed down with a cup of tea.

Now those feathers were smoothed, the Countess could withdraw to her boudoir to prepare herself for the festivities. Her dresser, Madame Boulversé, was going to be up in a minute, meanwhile she was immersed in throwing one silk gown after the other onto her four-poster bed, sighing deeply and incessantly shaking her head. She was entering a similar state of agitation as the maids downstairs, so had to call for the Count again.

The second *catastrophe* was solved when Guillaume returned with the cakes. He immediately had to reverse the T-Ford and drive Madame to *Le Centre de La Mode Moderne,* the flashy new department store that had recently opened in Roye, so she could purchase a much needed new gown.

"Beware of the third *catastrophe*," the Count told his green parakeet, in its golden cage in the corner of his own bedroom, while slipping into his best summer suit and donning a Boater straw hat on his head. He was most certain that a third *catastrophe* would come from one of his children. Only, which of the four?

"Not my Marie-Antoinette," the count told his parakeet. "She's the only one who takes after me, and shows some breeding. Pity she's too chubby and freckled to be much of a looker, but she may still grow out of her baby fat, and powders can do a lot these days."

He ventured over to the window with the tips of his fingers twirling his mustache. All four of them were on the lawn following the preparations for the gathering with great interest.

The footmen were placing tables and chairs, and setting up parasols. Others were placing baskets with flowers, and strung up paper garlands for decoration.

The Count's high forehead creased. His eldest, Elle, never got on well with her younger sisters, and also now they were obviously squabbling over something.

Though she was a dark-haired beauty with aristo-cratic features and exquisite eyes, she looked sour as she addressed her siblings. Marie-Antoinette and Madeleine were both still in their riding habits, and had clearly only just returned from their morning outride on their Arabian geldings.

Marie-Antoinette nervously tapped her boot with her whip, but little spitfire Madeleine had an accusatory look on a face very much like her elder sister. Her riding cap had fallen off her auburn locks and she balled her fists at her sister.

Much to his dislike the Count saw Elle put a cigarette between her red lips, turn her back on her sisters and stroll to one of the footmen – who quickly lit it for her. Swinging her hips she disappeared out of the Count's sight.

"That girl is trouble with a capital T," he told Belle, the parakeet, who immediately answered with a gurgling

"Trouble T". The Count's only son, Jacques, seemed unruffled by either the squabbles around him and the commotion that the tea party seemed to cause. As always he was lounging in his deckchair with a novel between his long fingers, a lock of dark hair covering half the young man's face.

"The 10th Count de Dragoncourt," Horace informed the parakeet, "is as a millpond. I can only pray to God that he won't be the last. And the good Lord knows we've had our share of troubles with the continuation of the lineage. We'll have to see what this new age will bring us."

～

MEANWHILE ELLE HAD COOLED DOWN from her run-in with her sister, who had apparently spotted her taking De Trémoille's car for a spin and threatened to tell Papa if she did not let Marie-Antoinette borrow her collection of gramophone records.

They were Elle's most treasured possessions so she'd really been in a dilemma, and this time that little brat of a sister had won.

Elle was so engrossed in her idea of becoming a race driver that she returned to the lawn to break the news to Jacques, the only one of her siblings she just pretended to hate but actually adored. The one thing that wasn't so great about him were his sudden fits of bookishness. For the rest he was quite dashing to see, popular with the girls, and the only one open to a bit of mischief like she was. Well, so was Madeleine, but she was still little more than a baby so she didn't really count.

Sauntering over to her brother, she started with a friendly,

"Hey, what are you reading?"

Her brother looked up, the dream of the story still lingering in his eyes.

"What was that? Don't be a hypocrite, Elle. You're not interested in what I'm reading. What do you want?"

It lay on her lips to disclose her secret to him.

Cars were all she could think about since feeling the Benz, but not having her plan ready yet– to yield her father into having a car designed for her – she bit her lip and said instead, "Do you know any of the people Mother and Father invited this afternoon?"

She sat down on one of the straight chairs that had been brought outdoors, pulling up her legs and hugging her knees.

While Jacques extricated himself from his own absorption to engage in conversation over the party with her, Elle was contemplating wearing trousers to the afternoon tea, not just for the shock of it but also to make a statement about her future career.

She was surprised to see the former glint of mischief return in Jacques' eyes as he said in a conspirational tone, "Well, I heard the eccentric Baron Dupuis de Melancourt is attending with his orphan daughter and her dog. Apparently, the orphan is quite a pretty thing and ever so unworldly." He winked at his sister. Yet, Elle had little interest in another of her parents' queer acquaintances and their appendages. However exotic at first sight, they always turned out to be shaped of the same dullness inside; their peculiarity just a veneer on their outward appearance while inwardly too afraid to move with the times, hanging on to their eccentricities as a lapdog to the hem of its mistress's skirt.

Elle sighed. Only thoughts of exhilarating speed and screeching tires seemed to make her heart beat faster. "I'm old before my years. I don't have a passion for people any longer," she declared dramatically.

"You never had, darling sister," her brother remarked sharply. "Passion equals possession in your case. In well-measured proportions."

Elle stuck out her tongue and softly muttered a cuss word. "Ah well, we'll have to survive another of these boring parties. Whatever, I won't be hanging out here for long. I've got other plans." She left Jacques, looking nonplussed.

"Hey, sis," he cried after her, "don't be a spoilsport. What are you talking about?"

"Racing, brother," she muttered under her breath, "and getting away from this dead spot."

But he didn't hear her.

5

THE TEA PARTY

S ome hours later as the first tones of Tobani's *Hearts and Flowers* resounded over the clinking of cups and light conversation, Elle came down the stairs resplendent in a white silk blouse and brown tie, and a pair of beige corduroy riding britches which hugged her slim figure at the waist and billowed out at the thighs. From the knee down her legs were clad in sturdy brown leather riding boots. Her hair was simply held together in a loose knot at the nape of her neck, with a brown male beret a little tilted on her pretty head. She had completed her outfit with very red lips and matching nail varnish. Liking the picture her mirror had reflected, she decided this new look befitted her new life – rendering dresses passé.

Anticipating the ripple of consternation her appearance would cause, she grinned widely, revealing strong white teeth that bit into an elegantly long cigarette holder.

"Thank you," she blew a kiss to De Trémoille who

hastened towards her to light her cigarette, adding under
her breath, "Toad."

Elle had missed the light-blue eyes of the girl sitting
in the shade at the outer ring of the gathering, holding a
leash in one hand while her other hand was lightly
splayed on the neck of the old dog sitting next to her.

∼

AGNÈS'S EYES were big with surprise. She had no idea
what to make of this person – *was it a girl?* – who had just
joined the party. Contrary to the rest of the attendees,
Agnès had no opinion on the newcomer's looks; it simply
confused her. She decided it must be a member of her
own sex because of the red nails and lips.

This girl obviously was part of the scenery as she
talked hither and thither, and everywhere she went was
approached with a mix of respect and bewilderment.

Agnès would have loved her father to tell her who she
was, but as he was occupied with his orchestra she sat on
her own, feeling excluded and isolated. Agnès wasn't one
for parties in general, but with her father not at her side
in these strange and unconventional surroundings, she
felt even more isolated and awkward. Still, she didn't
want to let him down and looked around her, trying to
pretend they were characters in one of her books.

She remembered all the things her father had told
her about this family, their wealth, and their special
Château. It made her decide to give them a chance, to be
tolerant and not so judgmental. Looking around she saw
there were more young people and children, so she
wasn't sure which ones were the Dragancourt clutch. A

group of young children was running around the lawn, while teenagers sat together at a table. The boy-girl also joined that group. Agnès sat alone with Gåva.

I doubt any of them will be interested in me, she thought with her usual withdrawn attitude, so she was surprised to hear a strong voice behind her exclaim, "Miss Agnès De Melancourt, or should I call you Miss Gunárssón?"

Her Swedish last name was pronounced in a singsong French accent. Agnès turned around to see a dazzling youngster come her way. He dropped himself on the empty chair at her solitary table and crossed his long legs.

The attractive young man started gazing at her from beneath a lock of black hair, scrutinizing light-brown eyes the color of medium-dry sherry. He proffered a slender hand, a signet ring dandily on his right pinky finger. Hesitantly, Agnès gave him her lace-gloved hand.

"Jacques," he introduced himself.

Nothing more. *So this must be one of the Dragancourt children*, raced through her head, but she wasn't sure. Every other male in France was named Jacques.

While she was still searching inside her vocabulary for the correct answer, he continued, "Well?"

"I beg your pardon?"

"What shall I call you?"

"It ... it doesn't matter, both are alright," she stammered, her cheeks coloring under his constant gaze.

Just when she wondered whether he would reveal if he was who she expected, he whispered in her ear, "I'm one of them!" Pointing his thumb in the direction of the Count, who was standing on the grass with his hands on his back listening to the *L'Esprit Musique*. "But I don't feel I am."

Agnès looked back at him without comprehending what he was implying. How could one not want to be part of one's own family? Family was so important, she knew all about that.

Also, from what she had gathered of the Dragancourt family from her Papa, they seemed a happy bunch with just the odd wild streak, but funny and accomplished.

So she asked, hesitantly, "Why not?"

Before he could answer she watched him stretch out his hand to Gåva. His movement was too abrupt, startling the old hound, who growled in response. A row of yellowed teeth showed under the lifted upper lip.

Jacques quickly withdrew his hand, uttering a surprised, "Heavens!"

"Gåva, down!" The dog immediately obeyed. With an apologetic look on her face, Agnès said, "I'm so sorry, Monsieur Jacques, my dog is blind and almost deaf, and very dedicated to me. She is also very protective of me."

"Never mind, my fault," Jacques assured her. "And please drop the Monsieur, unless you want me to keep *mademoiselling* you?"

He gave her an endearing smile, in which his rather dark features lit up and real handsomeness showed. Agnès thought his proposal quite forthright, so shortly after their acquaintance but as he still addressed her with the polite "*vous*" form, she nodded and smiled back, "*D'accord.*"

"Good," he said. "When we're with our *intima* we're quite informal here, as you can see." A long arm gestured to the people congregated on the lawns. Agnès,

with still his observation on her mind that he did not
want to be part of his own family, looked where he
pointed.

Jacques was right, besides the strange girl in the
trousers there were well-dressed ladies mingling with
people in exotic costumes, and children were running
wild and free in and out of the gathered groups. The
entire party had more of a random meeting in a busy
train station than an orderly afternoon tea.

Some people raised their voices to high volume,
women laughed throwing their heads back and almost all
of them, men and women, were smoking and hugging
each other freely.

This was not a sight Agnès was used to at her father's
gatherings at the Place the Châtelet. Papa wasn't formal
but he wasn't liberal either. There were certain standards
that all guests understood, even if they were unwritten.

People remained seated on their chairs, certainly
during musical performances, nor did they shout or
swear, and they didn't hang around each other's necks as
seemed customary here.

There was just one person who seemed almost like
her father's crowd and quite out of the ordinary in this
ensemble. He was a gray-haired tall man in a summer
costume, who was watching the musicians while twirling
his long mustache. Agnès guessed that he must be Count
Horace.

"So, why do you not want to be part of them?" she
ventured, not daring to specify *them* in case she'd misun-
derstood.

As she turned her gaze back to Jacques she saw his
brown eyes were burning into hers and she instantly

withdrew within herself, not knowing how to read this intense expression.

There was definitely a predatory undercurrent to him, and in all the people around her, which was making her increasingly uncomfortable.

Already regretting her candid question and scolding herself for trying to understand complicated relationships that had nothing to do with her, she tightened her fingers around Gåva's leash and looked down on them, avoiding his gaze. *I want to go home*, she thought.

The party was like a net thrown over everyone, as if they'd all become part of something she could only describe as frenzied infatuation. But with what, and for what reason, was a complete mystery to her. Her father's quartet was definitely not playing inciting pagan drums, but playful waltzes and lyrical tunes.

In the middle of her musings she heard Jacques say, "Forget about it, Agnès, I was only joking. They're not as bad as they seem."

She shot him a quick glance but his expression still had that focused intensity. It made her mind withdraw further, while her body tingled in a strange way, as if she too should throw something out in a loud way, or do something unheard of.

This was not the Agnès she wanted to be. Agnès wasn't wild, and never would be. She had no attraction to it. Let the warm-blooded French have their fiery emotions and let hers be as cool as a still lake in summer.

She tried to keep her gaze steady and unperturbed, and then watched him look away. Rather softly, he said, "Agnès and Jacques. No formality anymore. Now, can I get you a fresh pot of tea? This one looks quite cold."

"Please." She nodded, grateful the tension was broken.

The brown eyes flashed once more as he got up and she blushed but felt comforted for the time being.

She'd probably misjudged him. Gosh, she was so unworldly when it came to relationships, certainly with the opposite sex. Her cousin, Victor, was just a pal. He would never look at her that way. He was as shy as she was, their eyes never really meeting but instead focusing on the book they were reading, or the croquet ball they had to hit. For a moment she thought Jacques blushed too but she was sure she was wrong. Boys didn't blush.

Just when he got up to fetch the tea, the boy-girl came over to them with a cigarette hanging from her red lips.

She was staring at Agnès yet addressed Jacques, "Now, my brother, who's your latest conquest, if I may ask?"

She had her hands on her hips, standing at their table, square on her piece of ground, not budging one inch. *This must be Elle then*, Agnès thought, looking up at her with interest. Though some Parisian girls dared to dress quite extravagantly, she had never before seen a woman in trousers at a party.

The only time Agnès and Katell would wear jodhpurs was when they went riding in the Bois du Boulogne. But to a party? Never in a million years. It was not done, and yet Elle looked *ravissante*. Agnès had to admit it.

There was something so vivid and original about this girl. Agnès also sensed her unrest and dissatisfaction with something. Maybe she also didn't want to be part of *them*?

Jacques ignored his sister's remark and left the two

girls together, making his way over to the awning. Elle now returned her interest to Agnès.

"*Enchanté.*" The hand with the blood-red nails stuck out.

Agnès took the proffered fingers gingerly, and replied, "*Enchanté, Mademoiselle.*"

"I'm Elle, don't mademoiselle me *si'l vous plaît.*"

She sat astride on a chair, clearly enjoying the liberty her trouser-clad legs gave her in this position. "Soooo," she added in a slow, drawling voice, "you must be Agnès?"

Lighting another cigarette, she studied her through the smoke. It was very unsettling and frankly rude, Agnès thought.

Women didn't do that with one another. They talked, casting their glances aside. She just nodded and focused on the leash in her hands again. Gåva shifted her body at her feet, one eye half open, on the alert.

Agnès was glad Jacques soon returned with the tea and she was no longer alone with this weird creature. If she had to choose between the two, she thought Elle was more menacing than her brother.

This was a new realization that had not dawned on Agnès before now; that girls her own age could be intimidating. True, she had only been close to Katell, so did not have much comparison, but the sweet Île-de-Ré girl was in every way different from this worldly-wise woman.

With Katell, Agnès felt no barriers, they were always open and loving toward each other. They had never even had a quarrel. Papa always said they were like two peas in a pod. However, the situation only seemed to deteriorate after Jacques returned and poured her tea. Elle insisted on buttering a scone for her, and then brother and sister began arguing about whether the tea had sufficiently brewed.

"Don't fuss, Elle. I was looking after Agnès before you came along."

"Well, what did you tell me, brother? We had to investigate together. Remember?"

"Stop it. You're going too far." Jacques shot Agnès a quick look, shaking his head as if saying *don't pay attention to her*. But Agnès, though perhaps not as accomplished as them, was no fool and understood she had been the topic of discussion by the twins before her arrival.

Why that was so remained a mystery to her, but they had clearly now decided she was a competition to be dueled over. Well, if she had to choose a favorite there was no doubt it would be Jacques, so she smiled back at him – which set off Elle again.

"What have you two been smirking about behind my back?"

"Cool down, sis. Nothing has been done behind your back. I was just entering into a proper conversation with Agnès when you came barging in. I thought you said you had no interest in Papa and Mama's friends?"

Agnès was increasingly more uncomfortable, obviously being the tug of war between these two. She looked from brother to sister with an uncertain expression in her crystalline blue eyes.

The siblings had taken up position in opposite seats at her table, staring angrily at each other, with the grimness of two boxers in the ring.

There was a third creature she had to watch carefully

as well, and that was Gåva, who now sat upright, the hackles on her back slowly rising. Agnès was relieved to see the black evening jacket of her father's orchestra uniform weaving through the throng of people, coming their way.

"Here Papa," she cried, waving her hand in the cream-lace glove.

Max, on spotting his daughter hurried her way, his face widening in a smile when he saw her seated with two adolescents her own age.

"Ah *ma cherié*, how did we do?"

He was of course hinting at the concert just performed, but Agnès's non-musical ears, plus all the stifled emotion that had been going on around her, had failed to hear one note of the entire performance.

Fortunately, her Papa was more interested in her companions than her answer, and was already shaking hands with the twins. Finding out they were his friend Horace's children, he lost no time.

Without consulting Agnès, he said heartily, "You must come and visit us at Melancourt. Come this week! Unless you're busy. I can send the car any day you like." The hospitable baron insisted, "Don't you agree, Agnès dear? It will be delightful to hear young voices in our quarters once again."

The usually-so-observant father when it came to his daughter's needs somehow completely missed the dark cloud that slid over her fair features.

Inwardly she screamed. *No Papa!* But she did not dare to articulate it out loud.

On their way back home she would tell him about the disastrous meeting she'd had with the twins and that she had no inclination of becoming friends with them.

Her eyes were on Elle, who had now turned her attention from her to her father, staring at him with the same intensity in her topaz eyes.

"How far is it from here? I mean, your castle, Sir?" she asked with an angelic smile.

"I'd say roughly sixty miles. As the crow flies not more than forty, but it's all these winding roads and having to pass through the centre of Roye. We're just on the other side of the town."

"Sounds very pleasant indeed. What do you think, Jacques?"

Agnès held her breath, hoping he would decline the invitation.

She had to speak up now or it would be all arranged for her and there would be no backing out of it, but her tongue was glued to her palate.

"Sure," Jacques agreed, politely adding, "Thank you, Sir."

"Papa," Agnès began timidly, "didn't you say we wouldn't–"

But Elle cut in, "I could ask Papa to lend us his T Ford, then you wouldn't have to send the car for us."

"Why not?" Jacques said. "It's not like we're having a disastrously overloaded schedule right now, and Guillaume doesn't need the car every day."

"So that's settled then?" the Baron agreed, beaming at his daughter, who meekly smiled back.

She'd lost. There was no way out of it now. Not in a socially-acceptable way, at least. She wasn't angry with her father because she knew he thought this would please her. How wrong could he be?

"We'll be honored to come and visit, Sir. I'm sure you both will prove to be an excellent influence on me and my brother. And as my father would quote, *Un homme seul est toujours en mauvaise compagnie.* A lone man is always in poor company."

The Baron smiled, happy now that everything was arranged. Agnès among friends her own age during the summer.

"You're quite right, Mademoiselle Elle," he said in a chirpy voice.

No one heard the parakeet tweet on repeat, "Catastrophe, catastrophe!"

On their way home Agnès tried to talk her father out of the plan, but she could not come up with one solid reason to convince him. Ultimately she gave up her weakened defense and told herself to just hope for the best. After all, the twins would only be visiting for one afternoon. After that was over her peace would be restored.

She'd endure it. For her father's sake. Just once.

6

THE WEEKEND

Thus it happened that Jacques and Elle drove down the winding French lanes to Château De Melancourt, where Agnès awaited them with her chest constricted like a coiled cobra. Although they seemed a more normal pair of French youngsters as they crossed the drawbridge over the moat and Elle parked the T Ford with an elegant swirl at her feet. Many "aaahs" and "ooohs" escaped from the twin's lips as they looked up at the immense, four-feet thick walls. Agnès's shoulders lowered. Maybe it wouldn't be too bad.

Elle looked positively endearing in her fashionable Paul Poiret travel costume and Jacques had somehow managed to get his unruly locks into shape. He too had dressed in accordance with protocol, in a travel ensemble of moss green gabardine, with a beret in the same color donning his handsome head.

"What a delight!" the Baron exclaimed. "Agnès and I have talked of little else since the tea party. Welcome to Melancourt! I realize how old-fashioned this must seem compared to the splendor of Dragancourt, but we generally do not entertain here during the summer. We just like the place as it is, don't we, darling?"

After shaking hands with the Dragancourts, he pulled Agnès's arm through his with a gentle squeeze. There was no need for her to play a prominent role yet. Her father would take charge of that.

All the while her light eyes were scrutinizing the worldly couple. She decided that their more subdued looks were much more agreeable to the eye. Their manners seemed to have improved as well. Maybe this wouldn't turn out as awkward as it had first seemed. Maybe they just took more liberties at home.

The afternoon was rather delightful, with breezy conversation and ended with Elle accompanying the Baron on the grand piano. Max was thrilled to discover Elle had a good voice as she sang Wagner's *Liebestod*. Agnès listened with fascination. This version of Tristan and Isolde was her absolute favorite. She could have listened to that suave voice all day.

They played croquet on the lawn and Jacques let her win. Together they laughed and played, and the atmosphere was so light and merry that she had no qualms anymore, when Elle finally cried out, "Do come and stay with us for a weekend, Agnès. I would dearly love to go riding with you, and Jacques will perfect your croquet skills. Won't you, brother?"

"Of course," he enthused, "and I'd love to talk more about Henry James with you, Agnès. We seem to run parallels in reading the master."

Agnès looked to her father who was nodding with conviction.

She still wasn't convinced, something dark and dreary still tugged at her insides. The disastrous tea party still lurked in the back of her mind, but she had to admit this afternoon had been the best of the summer so far – so she consented. Only two nights away from Papa, and Gåva would be with her, of course.

"Great," Elle concluded. "Let's make it next weekend."

SOME DAYS later Agnès packed her overnight bag to venture on her sleepover at Dragancourt.

Gåva was restless, which brought up her own doubts again but the Baron was adamant the two of them would be just fine; that she would survive a short break from her tranquil life with him and the servants; that she could do with two days away from her books and her garden.

"Agnès, my darling, you and Gåva stayed with Katell's family on the Île-de-Ré for a fortnight last year. How can two days away at such a short distance be a problem now?"

"But Gåva wasn't as old then, Papa. What if she falls ill?

"They own at least five telephones, so I'll go down to Mr LeGrand to tell them that there might a ring from Dragancourt should anything. Then I shall come to collect you right away, or the Count will send you home with his chauffeur. Don't fret, my pet. Just enjoy the change of scenery."

~

AND SO IT was decided she would stay at Château de Dragancourt for the first weekend in August. Once again Agnès found herself in the fast lane of life at the Dragancourts, at the mercy of the terrible twins. She came to regret her impulsive consent soon after, but knew she now would have to sit it out.

Elle and Jacques at home were again their worldly-wise, cynical, and overbearing selves. Though only three years her senior, they were smoking constantly and talking about all kinds of liberal subjects, such as kissing the opposite sex, occasionally even using a crass word. And then there was Elle's manner of dress, and the fact that her parents permitted it.

I never want to be like her, Agnès thought to herself, *so I'd better take good note of how she behaves so I know what to avoid when I'm her age and go out in society.*

As if Elle guessed her musings, the wild one raised her topaz eyes from pouring her coffee. 'You're a bit of a snob, aren't you Agnès, behind that careful façade of modesty and character?"

"Elle!" Jacques protested when he saw Agnès cringe.

But Agnès was not a coward, so she straightened her posture and said through pursed lips, "I wouldn't know *that,* Elle, but I have my standards. It's not just how Papa raised me, it's also because I don't like curse words, and some topics I either don't know anything about or I think they're not decent for public discussion."

"Bravo!" Jacques clapped his hands with Elle looking even more sour.

"I believe in free speech," she snapped, lighting another cigarette.

Agnès had the distinct feeling Elle was unhappy and

that made her attitude towards this cynical young woman soften somewhat.

"Maybe you're right. Maybe I'm a bit of a snob." Agnès didn't even know if she'd spoken the words aloud.

Through her mind flashed the image of Elle singing at the piano, the way she'd looked up at the Baron and how her father had encouraged her with his warm smile. Elle had seemed happy then, much more her natural self than this angry person sitting across from her at the luxuriously set table in the Dragancourt garden.

Yet despite her decision to cut Elle some slack and concentrate on Jacques, Agnès's mental balance continued to be tested over and over that Saturday afternoon. She was glad to be able to withdraw to her guest room for the night to absorb all the contradictory impressions and write about them in her diary.

Like all rooms in the château, her room was a showroom of grandeur and opulence, but she and Gåva were too tired to pay much attention to their new surroundings. Agnès was glad that the still night soon wrapped them up in sleep.

Early in the morning there was a rap on her door, and she heard Elle called from the other side, "Wake up, lazy bum, we're going riding, or shopping, or racing the car around the lake. Or all three. I haven't decided yet."

~

AGAIN ON THE Sunday Jacques and Elle took over her whole life, while there was little sight of the other family members. Agnès saw only glimpses of the two younger girls. The Count was said to be away until Sunday night, while the Countess seemed to have evaporated into thin air. The three teenagers were left to themselves, spending all hours in each other's company. Much to the delight of Elle and Jacques, who got wilder and wilder, whereas Agnès fell silent, feeling trapped like a cat in a bag.

To Agnès this tempo was simply excruciating as the two lived at such a pace, and had such a short attention span, that they raced from left to right and left everything lying scattered in their wake; clothing items, croquet bats, riding boots, and books. It was impossible to keep up. Despite the increasing weariness and her longing for alone time, she was aware that the twins had an impact on her that was new, and exciting to some extent. The complete opposite of tranquil and organized for sure, threw her off balance but it also awakened something in her. Her body felt more alive, more vibrant, her mind followed suit, becoming more agile and adaptive.

She tried to steer clear from her haughtiness and attempted to see the good in this loud-spoken duo who had so much life and energy in them. Agnès's life reached a new wavelength. She was bobbing along and tried to let go of the strict reins on her vision of life.

After another long and dangerous car drive with Elle at the wheel, both Agnès and Gåva became carsick. Elle's driving style along the country lanes, combined with a large lunch, was too much.

"I need to lie down for a bit, and also calm my dog," Agnès said, as she stood in the courtyard in the blaring August sun. She was tottering on her two feet, only able to think of putting her head on her pillow for a moment and wind down.

"Alright," Elle said, looking as fresh as a daisy. 'I'll

take you to your room." The girls went up the stairs together, with Agnès carrying a limp Gåva in her arms, but when they stood outside the guest room door Elle blocked her way.

With her hands on her hips she declared, "You'd better rest in my room. It's more airy."

Too befuddled and tired, Agnès squeaked, "What?"

"I want to extend my hospitality to you and to be real friends. That guestroom is terribly drafty. My quarters are so cozy and there's plenty of space for us both."

"I don't know." It sounded doubtful.

Agnès put her dog down but held onto the leash. To be honest she had had quite enough of Elle for a couple of hours. She just wanted to rest in a dark room. At that moment Jacques came stomping up the stairs, obviously surprised to see them both standing in the hallway.

"What's going on? Someone seen a ghost?" he joked.

Elle shot her brother an irritated look. She had clearly not wanted his intervention in this new plan but was now forced to say something.

"Agnès doesn't feel well. I don't want her to be on her own in a strange room, so I've asked her to come and rest in mine?"

"Not necessary," Agnès protested weakly.

Jacques stared from one girl to the other, then grinned widely.

"Why not sleep altogether. Like in the old days?"

"I don't think so," Elle snapped. "Come on Agnès, time for bed." She took the bewildered girl by her hand and triumphantly dragged her along the corridor to her bedroom.

"Uh-oh," Jacques' voice sounded behind them. "Do I smell trouble?"

Agnès tried to worm her hand out of Elle's grip, but the harder she tried the more firmly the older girl tightened her fingers around hers.

"It'll be fun, Agnès, you'll see." Elle tried to make her voice comforting but it had the opposite effect.

This silent struggle went on until Gåva, who had been following her mistress closely, had had enough of it. Without further ado she dug her teeth into the heel of Elle's boot and did not let go.

"Ouch, stop that, dog!" Elle came to an abrupt halt.

Agnès was instantly torn. Her well-behaved decorum told her to give her dog the command to let go, but the foresight of being totally in Elle's clutches, out of sight of the other Dragancourt inhabitants, did not appeal to her. Her manners won.

"Down, Gåva!" The old dog obeyed immediately but her blind eyes went upwards to where she heard her mistress's voice, a vague wagging of the gray tail.

Elle looked more subdued now.

"I truly thought you wanted to come to my room instead of being on your own in that drafty guest room, but if you honestly don't want to see my luxurious quarters then feel free to return to your own dark corners."

"I'd rather," Agnès replied in her soft voice, "I really need to rest for a while. We'll see each other at dinner, alright?"

"Sure!" The topaz eyes squinted. "And we'll go swimming in the lake tomorrow morning before you leave. It'll be fun."

"I ... I didn't bring my bathing suit."

"Don't worry about that. I never wear one. We always swim naked. It's our own private lake. It's only the gardeners that can spy on us." Elle winked mischievously.

Agnès stared at her, aghast. In the background Jacques suppressed a snort.

"I don't think so," she replied primly, and with a grateful sigh returned to her own chambers. After closing the guest door behind her, she locked it immediately.

"What a weird girl," Agnès said aloud, and then set out to look after her exhausted dog. "You shouldn't bite our hosts."

Gåva's deaf ears accepted the reprimand with grace. The old dog went straight to her wicker basket and was asleep within seconds.

It took a long time before Agnès herself could rest, though her head pounded and her body was ready for sleep. Elle was fascinating, no doubt about that, and she felt that there was actually an insecure and lovely person under those layers of bombast, but one did not feel at ease with Elle de Dragancourt.

Her thoughts went to her friend Katell, who was now spending the summer with her grandmother at Île de Ré. She and Katell had been friends since they were seven, both orphans but for quite different reasons.

Katell had known her real parents when they lived in Saint-Martin-de-Ré, before they had both passed away from tuberculosis, weeks apart in 1900. Then Katell's grandmother had sent the young girl to Paris to live with her Aunt.

One day Agnès had seen the little girl, with the mass of copper curls, with a skipping rope on the Place de

Châtelet and they had naturally gravitated towards each other.

"Papa! I have a friend, Kat. She lives just across from us." Since then nothing could tear the two little waifs apart, only the summer holidays. Agnès sighed again as she drew the blankets to her chin. She missed Kat and she missed her father. So she sat up again and pressed the button on the electric bed lamp. What a luxury that was. This family had so many nice things. She really had to try harder to understand them.

"That's what I'll write about," she mumbled as she opened the dark-red leather binding of her diary, an annual present from her Papa.

～

AFTER HER REST there was another bout of driving on Elle's part. Agnès did not get Elle's infatuation with driving when she was dragged to the car for another spin.

She apparently only wanted to be at the steering wheel, maneuvering the T-Ford with generous swipes along the bends of the Avenue de Paris, until the multi-windowed Dragancourt castle with its extensive wings, like large arms holding the greenery in its embrace, became visible again.

"Enough hobbling around in cars for today, Elle," Jacques announced as they came closer to the majestic château at the top of the sloping grounds, lying almost gilded in the late afternoon sun. Turning around Elle glanced to the back seat where Agnès sat motionless with Gåva leaning against her, an unhappy frown on her pretty face.

"What would you like to do when we arrive?" Elle shouted over the noise of the engine.

"Aren't we supposed to have afternoon tea with Papa?" Jacques raised one eyebrow.

"Crap," Elle swore. "He must be back by now. He wanted to greet Agnès."

"When's Mother supposed to come back?" her brother asked.

"Not for another week, silly. She's off to Switzerland with De Trémoille. I told you so. Hanky-panky, the new lovebirds."

Agnès shuddered. Were they talking about their own mother openly having an affair? There was no end to the strangeness of this family. Then again, her father had told her there was something very libertine about the Countess.

Jacques must have sensed her growing mortification because he now turned his head to her while Elle concentrated on driving down the narrow driveway, lined with and avenue of trees that led to the castle's courtyard.

With a lopsided smile on his young man's face, he said in a conspiratorial way, "Never mind Elle, dear Agnès, she always tries to provoke. It's her second nature."

Elle stuck her tongue out at him but grinned. For once they were not fighting. Jacques' words did relax Agnès a little but she remained on guard, never knowing what the dark girl would blurt out next. It was as if a chunk of upturned earth tried to settle in her stomach area.

7

THE COUNT

Elle braked with a last dramatic screech of tires on the gravel of the drive that the Model T Ford came to a sudden standstill right in front of the castle's main entrance. She jumped out quickly to be the first to open Agnès's door before her brother had his chance.

Holding out her alabaster fingers to help her out, Gåva snarled at her. Elle quickly withdrew her hand. "Heavens dog, can you not behave for once? I'm only trying to help!"

Elle looked stricken, taking a step back. The reminder of the teeth in her boots a couple of hours earlier was clearly not forgotten. Agnès for sure had her bodyguard with her wherever she went.

The bodyguard's mistress had meanwhile lovingly picked her dog up in her arms and slid on her behind out of the car, where she put Gåva down. They both looked disheveled and out of sorts. The old dog shivered and yawned with a loud gasp. Again it was Jacques who tried to mollify her unease.

The lock of dark hair half over his brown eyes, his light summer suit somewhat crumpled from the many car trips of their day, he tried to pacify her by saying, "Come, let us go in and give you two a much-needed rest." His smile meant to give her courage but Agnès was past being mollified.

Walking up the stairs towards the entrance of the castle, she longed to make that phone call to her father with every fiber in her body. Suddenly it was all too much for her.

Flanked on both sides by the twins, one who tried to be nice and the other to just show off, only her lifelong companion that followed on her heels made Agnès put one step before the other.

∼

IN THE CENTRAL hall with the incredibly high ceiling, from which fat cherubs with harps and winding grapevines looked down on the world below, Count Horace de Dragancourt stood waiting for them. He had returned home from an unknown trip, leaving the four siblings in care of the staff while his wife was abroad with her lover.

Agnès had not really met the Count during the tea party, where they had only been shortly introduced to each other. Tall and stooped as if his heavy shoulders were weighing him down, she thought he looked older than the mid-forties he probably was.

His somber gaze fixed on the threesome, who were crossing the marble tiled floor with a querying expression on his clean-shaven, lined cheeks, as if he didn't really know if what he saw was actual reality.

Her father had told her Horace was the French ambassador in the United Kingdom, She thought he looked the part of a seasoned diplomat for sure, with his gray distinction and sharp steel eyes and wide moustache.

"Welcome to Château de Dragancourt, Mademoiselle de Melancourt," he said graciously, using only her father's name. "I'm sorry my wife and I weren't here to welcome you when you arrived. I do hope my lot is treating you well?"

He gave Agnès a small and uncertain smile while he took her hand. Fixing his steel-hued stare on the dog that was following her, without thinking twice he sank to his knees. "Oh, how wonderful, you brought your dog. How I miss my Bijou. My last Afghan hound died this spring. I still haven't had time to purchase a successor for her. What's your name, boy?"

Gåva, sensing an animal loving creature near, licked his hand and the hitherto dumbstruck Agnès found her tongue again. "Actually it is a she, Sir, and she's named Gåva. She's Swedish, like me." A shy blush colored the area under her cheekbones.

Horace got up with some difficulty, and swaying on his legs before he found his balance replied, "Ah yes. Your father told me as much, you being Swedish, how very distinct, very distinct."

Agnès knew how the acquaintance of the Count and

the Baron went back to the time that they were both students, but that their private lives were not really a subject of their conversations when they met for cognac and cigars at their Paris club *Arti et Amicitiae,* or during visits to the *Opéra National de Paris*, or in other circles they frequented.

She saw he tried to remember things like her father had done when he'd told her about Jacques and Elle. Both men really did not know much beyond their own amity with each other. Now she wished her father had done more research and would not have so lightheartedly let her come to this troubled place. All that she could tell was that the Count seemed blameless for the wildness of his offspring.

"Thank you for your invitation." She tried to make her voice strike the right tone. "Papa sends his regards."

"Let's try and find out where the devil the other children are hiding," the Count joked, and the youngsters trotted behind him.

Leading the small ensemble through a maze of long corridors and other halls, the Count finally opened an unadorned brown wooden door that looked like it had been installed in recent times. They entered a light room which was furnished with pretty walnut Queen Anne furniture. In the middle stood a long table with a white tablecloth, laden with cakes and fruits and sandwiches, akin to a proper English afternoon tea. Agnès remembered the mistress of the house came from Kent. The family was probably used to taking afternoon tea.

Comfortable leather chairs surrounded a low coffee table that overlooked the well-tended garden sloping down to the pond. The doors were open and white gauze curtains billowed outside in the soft afternoon breeze.

At least half a dozen paintings adorned the white-washed walls, a careful collection of the most well-known French impressionists; Renoir, Monet, and Cézanne. The floor consisted of a deep sienna mosaic parquet with rugs in off-white; fluffy and very soft to the toes.

"Please sit down," the Count invited. As soon as he rang the bell, a posh maid entered, carrying a Delft-blue china teapot with a reed handle.

The Count poured himself, then handed the cups around before he sat himself in the most worn leather chair, which sighed under his weight. It looked like he was the one using this room most often.

Agnès felt everyone could relax in this room. She felt more disarmed than before. Though the Count was much more standoffish than her own father, he breathed that same background and poise.

Suddenly Elle shot out of her chair and went up to her father.

She gave him a hearty peck on the cheek. "Welcome back, Papa, how very nice of you to be so kind to our new friend Agnès."

"By Jove, my child," the Count muttered, clearly taken by surprise at this unexpected show of his daughter's affection. "Come, let us all drink our tea in peace now and pray for no *catastrophes*."

Turning to Agnès, the elderly gentleman added, "You must excuse my wife and my other two daughters, Miss Agnès. My flock flies in all directions these days. It's hard to keep an eye on them all. A pity your dear father can't join us for dinner tonight."

Agnès thought he looked quite sad and lonely She bit her lip.

"Thank you, Sir. My father will be here tomorrow to fetch me so you'll possibly see him then."

"You're leaving so soon? I thought you'd be staying for another week?"

The Count looked surprised. Elle cut in immediately, "Of course, she will stay, Papa. The initial plan was only two days, but it's been such jolly fun that we can certainly extend Agnès's stay with another week. So much to do when Agnès is here. Jacques and I are suddenly no longer bored, and haven't been badgering the staff every other hour to let us return to Paris on our own before the summer is up."

"I'm glad to hear it," the Count said thoughtfully. "Agnès can stay as long as she likes."

Nobody noticed that all the blood drained from Agnès's already pale cheeks.

"No," she peeped anxiously, "I need ... I need to go home tomorrow." Not being able to think of any good reason, she came up with, "Gåva can't be away from home for too long. Look at her, she's exhausted."

All Dragancourt eyes went to the blind and deaf dog on Agnès's lap, and had to agree that her head hung limply and her rib cage was moving too fast from the stress.

"Just send her home to Melancourt then, Agnès," Elle suggested with her usual flair. "The old dog has been a ball and chain ever since you came here. It will do you good to be able to run around free of that burden for a bit."

Much could be demanded from the soft-hearted

Swede, but no one told her to separate from her dog. The blue eyes flashed ominously.

"Never!" It rang shrill and clear through the afternoon room. The willpower in her tone shocked her hosts, so she hastened to added a kindlier, "Gâva and I have not been apart for one day since I was born. She has always protected me. We need each other more than anything else in the world."

"Cut it, Elle." This was Jacques, his dark gaze warning his sister. "Let Agnès do what she wants to do. She's not *your* latest acquisition. I'm sure you're looking for a replacement for Westport?"

"Enough," the Count boomed. "I don't want to hear that man's name mentioned. What's the matter with you children? Instead of enjoying Agnès's company for another day, and hope she will return next summer or you two get an invitation to stay at Melancourt, you seem to want to spoil it by squabbling."

The Count looked unhappy, rubbing his hand wearily over his face before returning to his habit of twisting the tip of his mustache.

Elle shrugged and lit a cigarette. She demonstrably blew the smoke in her brother's direction. The atmosphere in the room was strained again. Gâva shifted her weight, opening one eye, on alert despite her frailness.

To break that tense ambience, the Count put down his cup with a bang.

"Does your father still have his rare collection of Chopin sheet music, Miss Agnès?"

Music not being her forte, but being brought up to converse well and steer around these lapses in the conversation, Agnès answered, "I suppose so, Sir. It was my grandfather who was *the* expert on Chopin. Sadly he passed away before being able to finish his biography on the great composer. Grandfather and Chopin were well acquainted. But you knew all that, I suppose?"

"Yes, your father told me he might finish the biography one day, based on your grandfather's notes."

"Do you play an instrument, Sir?"

"Oh my dear girl, I don't suppose your father will have regaled you with my attempts at mastering the piano. My efforts are in no comparison to his virtuoso. However, we do play the occasional Claude and Debussy together when we are at the club. Nowadays I feel rather embarrassed accompanying him, although I thoroughly enjoyed the performance with his orchestra during our afternoon tea party."

Agnès was glad to see that the memory made the Count smile, and the gray aura around him temporarily evaporated in a softer hue. It made his face light up. She could see he'd once certainly been as attractive as his children. They didn't have their looks solely from their ravishingly beautiful British mother.

Agnès felt a pang of sadness for the Count and somehow she also seemed to understand the unraveling of that family better. It also made her value what *she* had all the more.

A harmonious and loving relationship with her stepfather and a great friend in Katell. Agnès had always been content with her life. The former dark cloud of where she was born and how that place had swallowed her mother was outside the scope of her own memory, and therefore did not cast a shadow over her happiness.

"I hope you will come to Melancourt soon, Sir, to play the piano as my father plays the violin. You know music is my father's whole life. He misses being able to talk about it with someone. Sadly, I haven't inherited his musical genes." She smiled as she added, "Even if that had been possible."

"I will consider that seriously, dear child. Maybe we all will join in as a family. I'm really glad you're here. You're for sure a breath of fresh air at Dragancourt."

Elle was folded in a comfortable position in the lounge chair, her legs tucked under her while balancing the expensive cup of Darjeeling tea on the top of her right knee, from where it could drop and shatter with the slightest movement.

Agnès felt Elle was scrutinizing the pleasant babbling that went back and forth between her father and her. She cast the enigmatic girl a quick look.

Despite the cynical line around her coral-red lips, hard shelled Elle seemed to relax in that room while her father's kind voice sounded and the water of the large indoor fountain gurgled and splashed. Her beautifully shaped mouth curled into the tiniest of smiles. Following her gaze Agnès saw that as quickly as the face had lit up it darkened again. Looking across the room at her brother, Elle's eyes squinted. The smile disappeared as the sun behind a cloud.

Heavens, Agnès thought with exasperation. *These two are like cat and mouse.*

Elle banged her cup on the shining surface of the walnut tea table and got up to stretch. "I'm going to change for dinner," she declared. "Are you coming, Agnès?"

"Alright." Agnès got up pressing Gåva against her breast. "Thank you for the tea and the chat, Count de Dragancourt."

"The pleasure was all mine!" His crestfallen expression made her heart heavy.

8

THE DINNER

I n the Dragancourt household, with all its centrifugal forces, there was one aspect that bound them together like thieves, and that was the evening dinner.

Served on the stroke of eight in *la grande salle verte*, the family would unite there on a daily basis, together in place but not so much in spirit. Even if the kitchen maids, Daphne and Dolly, had another physical row during the day, there would be the customary five-course meal on the damask tablecloth with the Claret ready for Monsieur, and the Veuve Clicquot for Madame, who only drank Champagne all day long.

Guillaume stood right next to the entrance, wearing white gloves and a deadpan expression on his broad face. From there he could supervise the rest of the staff who were gathered to serve the main meal of the day to that assembly of odd yet age-old aristocrats.

None of the family members, not even Elle, would dream of not changing for dinner into more suitable formal dress, to sit down to the invariable joint of lamb or rolled pork. It was the one tradition that still had a semblance of old-school dignity.

Until the weekend when Agnès visited Dragancourt. Now even that semblance of unity was gone.

Never before had there been a public split-up between the Count and the Countess to the effect that she had packed her bags and openly left her husband to be with one of her *amants*.

In the Count's absence, Guillaume had taken the lead. Marie-Antoinette and Madeleine had been sent on the train back to Paris with their governess to be spared the disappearance of their mother.

Now the Count himself had decided to pack up early this summer and return for an indefinite time to his flat in London. Jacques and Elle would accompany him. With Agnès not wanting to stay, the summer in Picardy would be cut short.

None of this was known yet to either the twins or Agnès. To a random visitor the evening meal would just seem that fragmented family appearance was the customary thing here.

∼

ELLE HAD ESCORTED Agnès up the stairs but not insisted on coming to her quarters again. Gåva being at the end of her tethers after all the excursions and strain to keep her mistress safe, was Agnès's first priority.

"I'll feed her and get her settled," she said. "What time are we expected to go down to dinner?"

The night before she and the twins had camped out

in a small dining room close to the servants' quarters and there had no necessity for formal dress.

"Can I watch?" Elle seemed to jump at the occasion. "I love the bond between you and your dog?"

"Of course, but there's not much to it." Agnès opened her door, not expecting Elle to go off on a strange prank again.

It was always an intimate moment for Agnès to help her old dog with her dinner. She became more and more aware of how precious these moments were, so all surrounding circumstances had no place as she concentrated on her hound. She did not even think of Elle, slumping on her bed with the soft eiderdown duvet, watching the scene with fascination.

Everything Agnès did in that ritual was natural and self-evident. Talking to Gåva in Swedish, comforting and calming her best friend, she was simultaneously soothing herself.

"*Stilla, stilla, min äslkling,*" she kept repeating. "Be still, my darling." In the end Gåva ate a small portion of meat and drank a few sips of water that Agnès urged her to take, and settled down in her basket, too exhausted to protest. Only then did she think of Elle again.

"May I show you my rooms, now?" Elle jumped up energetically at the option to have Agnès finally to herself. "I promise I won't say silly things or make you do things you don't want to do."

No matter how frazzled she was with all the contradictions and odd goings on, she saw Elle trying very hard to be her friend. The dark girl bit her lip and looked so pleadingly at her that she consented. What could go wrong? It was not like Elle would attack her. And Agnès wanted to please her, some part of her felt pity with the devil-may-care girl, who somehow seemed lost in her own pranks.

"Okay," she agreed, "but how long do we have until dinner? I need to change and do my hair."

"Ages," Elle said carelessly, "your hair is fine. I bet there's never one hair out of place on your head and you just slip on the first dress in your cupboard, et voilá! Now come!"

Throwing a last glance at the sleeping dog, who did not seem to stand in her way this time, Agnès followed Elle down the corridor.

They entered a very opulent room for an eighteen-year-old girl. Agnès had never seen such extravagance and for a moment could not rhyme it with the nonchalant, boyish figure of Countess Elle.

In the first room was a double bed with a ribbed white quilt tightly tucked in. Next to it was a side-table and a lamp with a green shade, and loads of draperies and big cupboards. They went through a pass way, of what apparently was Elle's master bedroom. Her bed was an impressive mahogany four-poster with matching tables on both sides.

The rest of the room contained an out of proportion wardrobe which obviously housed Elle's extensive wardrobe, as many articles had escaped from drawers and boards, and lay crumpled and forgotten across the thick beige carpet. Lamps were lit everywhere as the heavy fawn velvet curtains were drawn, which gave the room a nightclub-like atmosphere as no outside light could filter through the drapes.

For the rest there was an odd jumble of chairs and

tables that seemed to have been knocked over at some instance but then put upright again, not knowing exactly what their original positions were.

After looking around the room, as there was no way her host could show her around, there being obstacles everywhere on the floor, Elle preceded her to an en-suite bathroom with gilded taps and an entirely mirrored wall.

Also here, Agnès was quite affronted by the mess of tubes and bottles spread everywhere, even a beige slip with lace trimmings was lying on the floor instead of in the laundry basket.

Agnès honestly asked herself how Elle could not be embarrassed to show her this eruption of personal belongings, but the owner and creator of the eruption was quite unperturbed. She simply added to it by stepping out of her afternoon dress, a low-cut crimson mousseline piece of nothing, without any brace or lining.

Standing in front of her guest in her equally red corset, whilst studying herself in the mirrored wall that multiplied her sparsely dressed reflection in layer after layer, the red lips mocking. Elle's hands piled her black hair on top of her head and striking a seductive pose, seemed to enjoy seeing Agnès's color also turn the same deep-red as the garment. Yet Agnès was unable to avert her eyes from the exposure of so much nonchalant beauty.

Elle, seeing she finally had Agnès's full attention, couldn't help herself and pushed the line. "I need to change my underwear as well as I'm to wear a silk dress tonight and this red garment would be seen through the white silk. So..."

She unfastened the hooks of her corset and stepped

into her Eve's ensemble without so much as blinking one eye. Agnès rushed out of the bathroom, appalled. She looked around the room, wanting to escape from the house and this girl immediately, but because her beloved dog was lying in the other room, probably fast asleep, she sat down on the bed in the room adjacent to Elle's bedroom, She waited in anxious worry, chewing the inside of her cheek.

Minutes later Elle reappeared from the bathroom wearing a silk silver dressing gown pulled tight around her figure, and looking more morose than Agnès had expected.

"Sorry Agnès, I don't know what it is that I always need to provoke people, like Jacques says. It's not that I like to be this way. Can you forgive me?" Elle lit a cigarette from her silver cigarette case, She inhaled the smoke deeply.

Her gold-flecked eyes, definitely one of her most attractive features, gazed on Agnès who was still sitting on the bed, her arms folded defensively over her chest. She didn't answer.

Elle let herself fall next to her on her bed, the robe falling open, disclosing her tanned thighs.

"I could really do with a friend," she said to the ceiling of her anteroom, tipping the ash into the ashtray she had mounted onto her tummy. Still no answer from Agnès. "I know I'm not a good person, Agnès dear, not the kind of person who inhabits your world, but I'm not all bad, believe me. I have a dream, a real dream that I think would turn me into a better person, a more caring member of society, but I have no idea how to go about realizing it. It's haunting me day and night..." Her voice trailed off and she turned her gaze to the closed curtain as if she wanted to look through it and see the world beyond.

Agnès didn't know if she was supposed to say anything or had to wait until Elle resumed her soliloquy. The reality was that it was no soliloquy.

"I want to become a race car driver."

Despite herself this made Agnès chuckle. "You want what?" She looked at the girl and saw a tear stream down her cheek. "I'm sorry, Elle," she added, "I just don't understand you, I guess."

Elle waved her hand with the scarlet nails. "Never mind, Agnès! Now get dressed. Unlike you, I'll never be anyone special."

"Don't say that," Agnès replied. "I don't know that I'll ever be anyone special either."

Elle got up and tied the dressing gown tighter around her,

"Of course you will, Agnès Gunarsson de Melancourt. The world will be licking your toes one day. Mark my words. But I will not be a part of it. Now go to your room, I'll try not to upset you anymore. I just hope I can curb my stupid actions. I'll knock on your door in half an hour. Okay?"

∾

AGNÈS QUICKLY DRESSED in a light-blue brocade with a charming band in the same color that she placed on her golden locks. But while she studied her reflection in the mirror she felt as if the heaviness of this family was weighing her down.

"Be someone special," she told her reflection. "And what would that be?"

Papa had told she could become anything and anyone she wanted. It was *her* choice. If she wanted to marry young, or go to university, he would not stand in her way.

"I want to mean something to other people," she declared, and it surprised her.

Other people had never played a big a role in Agnès's life. She had no idea what it would be but she wanted to help people who had less than she had.

When Elle rapped on her door, she opened with a smile. Elle looked surprised. Linking her arm through hers, Agnès said, "Thank you, Elle, for teaching me a thing or two."

"Me?" Elle's grin was as wide as the Champs Elysees. "You're not serious?"

"I am!"

Arm in arm they descended the stairs to make their way to *la grande salle verte*, the heels of their evening shoes clicking rhythmically on the marble floor.

In the large dining room they found Jacques, dressed in a double-breasted black dress suit with a white waistcoat. He quickly came over to them to secure a place on Agnès's right side, but Elle stepped in quickly. She changed the plates around so she would be on Agnès's left instead of having their guest sit next to her father.

Guillaume, who oversaw the serving of the family at dinner, had already taken up his usual position and stood stiffly upright next to the gilded doorpost. He frowned as this messing with the plates would lead to confusion among the maids, but he refrained, as always, from making a remark, so as not to further inflame the already volatile atmosphere at Château Dragancourt.

Agnès accepted Jacques's help to get her seated. As a result she was the first one sitting at the huge oval dining table, above it two chandeliers which sprinkled a gay light from a myriad of pear-shaped electric bulbs over the white damask cloth.

Unlike the former Agnès, this new Agnès was very aware of all the bustle that was going on around her in the green room; the luxurious display of food and crystal, expensive china, and the gallery of portraits. She felt no longer afraid of these strange surroundings.

What was there to be afraid of? It was all a lot of ado about nothing. She decided that she would cherish her life with Papa even more after she returned to Melancourt. When they took up residence again in their house in Paris in the autumn, she would seriously look into studies that involved helping others.

Agnès was adamant she would not waste one minute of her happy life together with her father and Kat, no matter how uneventful that life may seem to others.

Jacques on her right was trying to get her attention so she shook off her future life plans to listen to him.

"Don't you agree that the way James portrays Kate Croy's desire to marry the penniless Merton Densher is a superb description of a doomed love affair, it's ..."

Agnès fixed him with her light-blue eyes. "You really *are* reading *The Wings of The Dove*?"

Jacques seemed somewhat taken aback by Agnès's doubt in his literary honesty.

"Well, yes," he answered cautiously. "Reading it at present."

"So am I!" Her enthusiasm for a kindred spirit in her love of books was easily kindled, "Isn't it brilliant? The subtleties of love! Why, there are so many aspects that can make people believe they are in love when in reality it is something else they're experiencing, like possessiveness or loneliness."

Agnès suddenly sounded very mature. She was aware she was speaking of something she had no notion of in reality. However, she loved theoretical concepts and discussing them. It felt for a moment as if she was discoursing with cousin Victor.

She was meanwhile also aware of Elle's eyes resting on her with that peculiar look she couldn't decipher, but which made her uncomfortable. As if Elle wanted to take possession of her. So she concentrated on Jacques, who was much easier to talk to. Then, from the corner of her eyes, she was glad to see the Count at the head of the table was enjoying their conversation too.

"Indeed," Jacques' dark lock bobbed agreeingly. "That's what I admire most in Henry James. Apparently the author himself is adamant he will never marry, but he is ever so skilled in laying bare the human deceptions to choose a life companion of the opposite sex."

Jacques cast a quick glance at his father, which both Elle and Agnès did not miss.

"If I ever marry it will be out of love and nothing else," Agnès proclaimed rather shrilly and with more force than any of her earlier utterances. The vehemence of her declaration brought a flush to her fair face.

From under her eyelashes she peeked at her handsome table companion. He was nodding in an absorbed way, as if what he was hearing was the wisest thing anyone had ever uttered in *la grande salle verte*. It gave her a funny, fuzzy feeling.

The evening ended more pleasantly than she'd so far encountered at Dragancourt. One more night and she would be going home.

9

THE FLIGHT

After the meal, Agnès soon asked to be excused as she was very tired, with a slight headache, She longed to think through her thoughts and be close to her dog whom wasn't used to being alone in strange surroundings.

Falling asleep instantly, forgetting all that had upset her and all she'd learned, she slept the rosy sleep of healthy young people.

She woke with a start, feeling the bedclothes move. It was still night, or at least it looked like it as all lamps had been extinguished and it was pitch black around her. It didn't take her two seconds to realize Elle had slipped into her bed and that she was completely naked, pressing her body tightly against Agnès's back. She had forgotten to lock the door!

"Get out of my bed!" Agnès yelled, startled and angry, yanking the bedclothes around her. But Elle pressed a hand over her mouth and stifled her cries.

Agnès struggled, trying to free herself from Elle's firm grip, but the older girl was stronger.

"Shhh ... Agnès, I didn't mean to frighten you. I was just so cold and lonely in my own bed."

Agnès thought that was the craziest thing she'd ever heard in her whole life. Be cold and take all your clothes off! Elle was truly deluded.

She tugged at the arm that was held in front of her mouth and then Gåva was on the bed too, snarling at Elle who immediately dropped her attack and lay still.

Agnès switched on the bedside lamp. When light flooded the room she was able to calm her dog. But it took some time.

Elle lay panting on her back with her eyes closed, as naked as God had made her.

"Are you out of your mind? I'm going away from here right now," Agnès struggled out of the bedclothes and started dressing herself over her night clothes. In her haste she tore off a button here and a ribbon there, but she didn't care. Enough was enough. This girl was unsound and had no morals.

Agnès was dressing herself so frantically that she didn't see that Elle moved to the door with catlike grace and locked it, holding the key triumphantly between her red-tipped fingers.

"Come on Agnès, don't be a spoilsport," she begged. "I just like you so much, you're so special. I honestly believe I've fallen in love with you. I shouldn't have climbed into your bed. Come on, I promise it won't happen again. Will you please, please not make a fuss now?"

The topaz eyes flashed beseechingly, and she went to the bed to throw her silver dressing gown around her as a sign of good behavior. Agnès was revolted by so much brazen action. She was determined to leave that very minute. From the little she'd seen in this household there was no one reining in the wild Elle, so that left her without another option.

"I just want to go home." Agnès's voice was flat. "You lot are not my style."

"I know." Elle sounded defeated, deflated. "I always spoil everything. But think of Jacques, he will be so sad if we part ways in disagreement, and what will your dear Papa think?"

"Disagreement?" Agnès was really angry now. "You attack me in my own bed, make advances towards me, almost suffocate me and then you call it a 'disagreement'? I'm really done here."

"But what about Jacques?" Elle tried again, her head hanging.

"He will understand. He knows you better than anyone else. And he knows your pranks. Now please just open the door and let me go."

"It's four-thirty in the morning, how on Earth will you travel the sixty miles to Melancourt at this time of night? It isn't even light yet."

Agnès chewed the inner side of her left cheek, a habit she had when at a loss. She just wanted to leave Dragancourt to never return to the place again. She didn't want to see any of these people ever either.

"I will sit on the steps and wait until Guillaume awakes, and then I'll ask him to telephone my father."

"Don't be such a milksop, Baroness Agnès."

It was said in such a demeaning way that for the first time ever Agnès's anger flared up beyond her control. She closed the distance between them. Then punched Elle in the face. Elle staggered back, her eyes filling with tears as she grabbed her bleeding nose. Agnès's knuckles burnt.

"Whatever you think of me, I'm not a milksop, Elle. Neither am I a coward!"

Without knowing what she did she hit Elle again across the face, and the girl fell sideways on the carpet, banging her head against the post of her bed.

She lay motionless. Agnès panicked. Her knees became wobbly and weak. Had she killed her?

But she saw Elle move, then curl up in a ball. With eyes closed, she kept lying like that. A beautiful dark Siren, lost in herself.

Without knowing what to do next, Agnès picked up the key that had fallen on the ground, and grabbing her bag called Gåva to follow her along the corridor, tears stinging in her eyes. Not seeing where she was going until she bumped into Jacques. He'd clearly awoken from the noise and was coming to see what was going on.

Agnès stammered incoherent words, sobbing loudly, but in the end Jacques could make out what had happened and soothing her tried to make her sit down, but there was no reasoning with the distraught girl anymore. It was as if Elle's wildness had transported over to Agnès.

"I hate her, I hate her!" she kept repeating.

So in the end Jacques wrapped Agnès in one of his own jackets and with rattling teeth, carrying the shivering Gåva in her arms, drove her back to her father's château in the T Ford, while the first rays of light glimpsed over the rolling hills.

"I am so sorry about all this, Agnès. I do hope you

believe me?" He only broke the silence when they were slowly entering the driveway to the Melancourt estate.

"I do, Jacques. You've been kind to me. And I know Elle can't help herself." It sounded small and muffled.

"What in the world will your father think, you coming home at this odd time and without being properly dressed?"

"I'll tell him I fell sick and you had to bring me home in a hurry."

"I'll bring anything you left behind, and Gåva's things, in the afternoon, okay?"

"Thank you, Jacques. Thank you and goodbye."

"I guess it will be goodbye for good?" He sounded just as sad as his father.

"Yes, Jacques. I know I shouldn't have hit Elle. Your father will be so angry with me."

"Not at all. Honestly, I think he'll thank you for it. You're actually the first one to put Elle in her place."

"I'd rather not be that person, Jacques. You're all just a tad too different from me."

They stood looking at each other. Agnès thought he looked terribly young and uncertain in the early morning light. Tentatively she put out her hand. He took it eagerly.

"I hope," he said, his voice coarse as if grating against a jagged lump in his throat, "I hope that one day our paths will cross again and we'll both be more mature and freer to choose our ways through life. Until then I'm going to miss you, Miss Agnès. You've been a beautiful ray of light in what has been a drab and soulless summer. *Au revoir*, and let nobody ever change who you are. You're beautiful."

She watched as he got behind the wheel, Gåva

clinging to her, and as she watched the black car slowly disappear among the sycamore trees, for some reason Solveig's Song floated into her tired head;

the summer too will vanish and then the year.
But this I know for certain: thou'lt come back again.

∼

AS THE CAR took a bend and disappeared out of sight, Agnès turned to face her parental home, her moist eyes blurred by the soft morning light. Slowly she made her way across the courtyard, where she felt for the key under the flowerpot. Pulling Jacques' coat closer around her slender shoulders, she slipped into her father's house. Safe for now.

∼

THANK YOU SO MUCH for reading **Miss Agnès**, *the novella duet that was an inspiration for* **The Resistance Girl Series**. *There are another novella,* **Doctor Agnès**, *and 8 books in the big series!*

I'm thrilled you've read the first novella. Your enjoyment of my stories about Resistance Women in the World wars means the world to me and I hope you'll continue to read all 7 books.

BUT WAIT, THERE'S MORE!

As a token of my appreciation, I invite you to join my exclusive newsletter community. By becoming a part of my inner circle, you'll gain access to exciting extras, promos, and a FREE novella - **The Partisan Fighter** *- an exclusive companion story to* **The Resistance Girl Series** *you won't want to miss.*

DON'T LET THIS OPPORTUNITY SLIP BY – *immerse yourself in my WW2 world of resistance, courage, and passion by unlocking*
  The Partisan Fighter here.
  Print: www.hannahbyron.com/newsletter

WARMEST REGARDS,

Hannah Byron

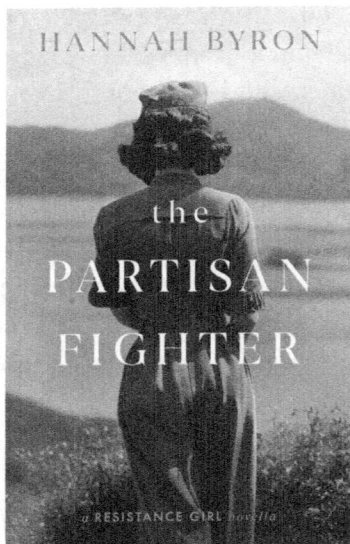

SNEAK PEEK IN PICARDY'S FIELDS
CHAPTER ONE TWO MEN

Paris, March 1918

The late afternoon sun set ablaze the upper windows of the operation room in the Lycée Pasteur, creating a golden aureole over the electric lamps that illuminated the wounded soldier on the table and the medical staff around him. There was a concentrated silence in the room, interrupted only by the faint hissing of the Heidbrink anesthetizer gas machine and the short commands Professor Alan Bell issued from behind his surgical mask: *Harmonic scalpel ... retractor... lancet*, which were promptly handed to him by the American nurse at his side.

From the other side of the table, the young assistant doctor Agnès de Saint-Aubin followed the surgeon's swift and practiced hands as he removed the bullet from the patient's neck. There was an intense, steady focus in her blue eyes.

"*Voilà!* Another 5mm bullet from those bloody G98s."

For a moment, Dr. Bell studied the round ball between his tweezers before depositing it in a metal tray that the nurse held ready. It clattered, metal hitting metal.

"More oxygen... antiseptics!" The surgeon had already moved to the next stage.

Agnès knew how complicated and dangerous this gunshot wound was. It had hit the young French soldier at high velocity, and the trajectory of the bullet had damaged his nervous system. He was bleeding profusely and was greatly in need of a blood transfusion, which another nurse was hastily preparing. With the strong medicinal odor of the chlorine prickling her nostrils, Agnès let her gaze rest for a moment on the young man's still profile, the roman nose, the dark, almost girlish eyelashes over his closed lids, black locks of matted hair emerging from under his operation cap. He still retained a vague glow of health under his ashen color. How old was he? Seventeen, eighteen? What had he dreamt of achieving in this war? And what would become of him now?

"Stitch him up, Doctor de Saint-Aubin, and when you're done, come and see me in the canteen."

Agnès startled. Her eyes met those of her American professor, and she thought she saw a softening in the steel-gray gaze.

"Of course, Professor Bell, right away." Her words were more straightforward than her voice, but she hastened around the table to take up his position next to the stout nurse. The head surgeon had already removed the white cap from his brown curls and was now snapping off his surgical gloves. With his gaze still on Agnès, he gave his last orders to the nurse.

"Nurse Simpson, assist the new doctor. Make sure you check her multilayer sutures. Nurse Belliard, blood transfusion – now!"

"Yes, Professor Bell," both nurses answered, while Agnès took a deep breath and ceased following the movements of her professor to give all her attention to the young patient on the table. His life; not hers.

She heard him disappear through the swinging doors that flapped for a couple of times before falling still. Agnès took another deep breath, steadying her hands before she said in a subdued voice, "Needle..."

The American nurse, ready to exert a maternal preponderance over this inexperienced doctor, instantly handed her the bent needle and thread. In an upbeat voice, she added, "You'll do all right, Doctor."

This kind nudge gave Agnès the confidence she needed, and she completed the complicated sutures under the older woman's scrutiny, knowing she was doing the best job at stitching she had done so far.

While she was washing her hands at the enamel sink in the kitchen unit next to the operation room, she heard the screeching wheels of the hospital bed as the patient was wheeled to the recovery room. She hoped he would live and convalesce completely but knew his chances were slim. So many had already died under her hands. She reminded herself of the next step in the process; no more thinking of the patient at this point.

She should be proud. She had done well, blocking her emotions during the operation and especially during her own suturing. She was making progress. Professor Bell's lessons were finally sinking in; she was developing a neutral attitude to suffering and complications. Agnès smiled at herself. She could hear him say it in that American tongue of his, pronouncing his r's and long, drawling vowels, an English so exotically different from that of her Oxford English tutor.

"Doctor de Saint-Aubin, there is no difference between a male and a female surgeon. Emotions simply stay out of the operation room. Always."

Drying her hands on the blocked tea towel, she wondered what his reason was for summoning her to the canteen. They had never met outside the lecture room or the operation theater, so Agnès felt uneasy. She was mastering the work; simply doing the job, identical to cutting and stitching dummies during the lectures. Truth was that her stomach still felt queasy after every operation – no matter that Professor Bell had told her she was cut from a special cloth; that female surgeons were going to be the stars of the twentieth century. He had taken it upon himself to personally supervise her surgical progress after she obtained her *Diplôme de l'Etat de docteur en medicine* from l'Université de Sorbonne in the spring of 1914; first at the American Hospital in Paris and now as part of his operation team at the Lycée Pasteur. Nothing pointed to him being dissatisfied with her. So, what now?

She suppressed a sudden thrill that he might ask her out. There had never been anything but a professional contact between them, and he was – of course – almost a decade older than she was, somewhere in his early thirties.

"Silly goose, he's probably married. Although he doesn't wear a wedding band. But who does in the operation room?" As she smoothed her springy blonde hair on top of her head and gave her full lips a dash of coral lipstick, she noticed how pale and tired she looked, with dark rings under her eyes, her face pale from the rationing and working long hours. How would he ever notice her if she looked so mousy? To add some color to her cheeks, she gave them both a soft pinch, and then gazed at her own eyes. They were an intense soft blue; *robin's egg blue,* Papa called them. If only she looked a little darker, more French – which was a ridiculous wish as everyone always complimented her on her pale, elflike look. But the Americans loved the dark-haired French girls. She saw it all around her.

Smoothing the dark-green pleats of her day dress, Agnès hastened through the long corridors of the Lycée Pasteur, originally built as a school for Neuilly-sur-Seine but now temporarily turned into an extension of the American War Hospital because the ongoing war demanded more emergency beds every day. Temporarily? It had been going on for close to four years now, and it only seemed to get worse. Outside in the Lycée's court-yard, the blue vans of the American Ambulance Field Service came and went in parade, with never a lull in the arrival of wounded men from the front. But for today, her day at the operation table was over.

Before entering the canteen, Agnès paused for a moment. Doctor Bell had always been honest with her, so there was no reason to think she had muddled things up. Chin up, she told herself.

The hospital canteen was the only place in the 1600-bed hospital that offered a relatively warm space to relax and recuperate. It was a large, whitewashed room with a high, beamed ceiling and a row of tall alcove windows along the Boulevard d'Inkermann letting in plenty of light during the day. Around the clock, the canteen was a beehive of comings and goings, filled to the ridge with the smoke of hundreds of pipes and cigarettes, the chatter of voices, the clinking of cutlery and the scraping of wooden chairs over the sanded floorboards. On both sides of the long tables, the electric bulbs above them looming as oversized pearls, a variety of nationalities sat side by side. Medical staff, ambulance drivers, recovering soldiers, they all shared just one goal: to win the war against Imperial Germany.

Agnès saw Alan Bell standing near the soup table, engrossed in animated conversation with one of the pretty American Red Cross nurses. His hand touched her arm lightly at times, and he nodded at her while the brunette gazed up at him, recounting what must have been a funny story as they both laughed heartily. Hesitantly, Agnès approached, not sure whether she should interrupt their conversation, but Alan spotted her and gestured to her to come closer.

"Doctor de Saint-Aubin, come and meet Elsie Gamble. She's from Chicago, like me! We grew up on the same street. Now, isn't that a coincidence?"

Agnès noted how he called the nurse by her first name while addressing her formally, but when she shook the girl's soft white hand, Elsie smiled warmly.

"So nice to meet you, Doctor de Saint-Aubin. I won't tell you all the good things Al's just told me about you." *Wink, wink.* "I'm ever so impressed to meet a female surgeon in the flesh. But right now, I should get my lazy behind out of the way, as my shift's starting in ten minutes."

With an amicable slap to Alan's arm, she moved away.

Her round hips swayed slightly under her white nurse's coat, a fact that did not go unnoticed by the soldiers in the room, whose weary faces brightened whenever they caught a glimpse of female beauty. Just like the Americans and Brits liked the French girls, the Frenchmen were infatuated with American nurses, who were known to be ever so carefree and spontaneous.

"Sit over there." Alan pointed to a table in the corner that was slightly less crowded. "I'll get us something. Would you like some soup, or toast with scrambled eggs?"

"Just a café au lait and a biscuit, please."

Alan looked at her with one dark eyebrow raised. "Still not steady on the nerves? I won't insist, but after eight hours at the operation table, you do need to eat a little more than a cookie, Doctor de Saint-Aubin."

"I will, in a minute. But first, coffee. And please, call me Agnès."

She watched him order himself a full plate of beef bourguignon and a large mug of tea. He moved with such ease, such composure, speaking French to the fat cook as if he had lived in her country all his life. It had become second nature to her – minutely studying his expressions and movements – but so far it had only been a logical process of learning from him in the operating theater. As this was the first time seeing him interact with others outside the medical sphere, it was a novelty to her but she studied it all just the same.

He came towards her, balancing his food and her coffee on the metal tray, and she noticed the smile had disappeared from his handsome face.

"I'm ravenous," he announced. "I do have something

important to tell you, but could it wait a couple of minutes until I've wolfed this down?"

"Of course." Agnès stirred her coffee, steadying her queasy stomach against the strong smell of beef that wafted her way. She intentionally diverted her attention to other people at their table to stop herself from scrutinizing him. When he had put down his fork and wiped his mouth on the linen napkin, her eyes met his again. She was aware she must have looked puzzled, but she could not read his intentions. He seemed to be struggling with something, and for a moment, her heart thumped in her throat.

"I'll call you Agnès if you agree to call me Alan." His voice had lost the professorial tone, but it was flat and devoid of emotion.

She nodded, waiting.

He took a sip of his tea as if weighing his words. "I wanted to tell you that I'm leaving Lycée Pasteur to move to a base hospital at the front."

She still did not reply, but looked down at her coffee cup to hide her disappointment.

"There are two reasons for this, Agnès. The first is that I want to make a real difference in this war – to give it my all, saving lives where it matters most. And secondly, I want to study the major leaps in medical progress where they really happen. And that's at the front. The war is proving to be a great teacher to us doctors."

With some difficulty, Agnès raised her head again. "Why are you telling me this?"

He gave a short, dry laugh. "I didn't just want to disappear. It didn't seem right. You've been my student for four years, and I've been your practical supervisor for the past year. So, the time is right. You're ready to take over from me. You're a good surgeon, Agnès."

"I want..." she started, but then stopped, diverting her gaze again. An awkward silence crept up between them. "I'd like some scrambled eggs on toast now."

"Good choice." He jumped up, giving her space to collect her thoughts. Although she had seen dozens of Allied surgeons departing to the field hospitals closer to the front, it had not occurred to her that Alan might go as well. After all, he oversaw the entire operating team in Paris. But everything was changing. Maybe he was right. Maybe she wanted to go too, and be where she could make a real difference, help the heavy casualties, save lives on the spot.

Agnès's brain worked hard. It was not the first time she had thought about going closer to the battlefields. When the war started, her father and she had made plans to turn their château near Roye into a field hospital, but the Germans had prevented that by seizing the castle during the First Battle of Picardy in September 1914, and since then, its medieval fate hung unknowingly in the air.

Alan returned with her meal and suggested she take her turn eating while he smoked a cigarette.

Having made her decision to ask him to take her with him, Agnès picked up her knife and fork. "You're not in a hurry?"

He waved his hand, dispersing the smoke. "No, not at all. Got all evening. I planned to take a walk along the Seine. Could do with some relative peace before the real madness starts. Care to come along?"

Agnès smiled. "I'd love to!" She had eaten a few bites and pushed her plate aside. Resting her elbows on the tablecloth, she asked in her quiet voice, "Can I come with you to the front?"

For a moment he seemed baffled, then curtly said "No!" while extinguishing his cigarette in the overfull ashtray with a firm jab.

But Agnès was not that easily pushed aside. "Why not, Alan?" Saying his Christian name was an unusual experience, but it felt invigorating.

He jumped to his feet. "Let's take that walk, and I'll explain why."

From the Lycée Pasteur, they walked along the rue Peronnet in the direction of the Seine. The March sun had already sunk behind the tall buildings, and leaden clouds gathered in the sky signaled rain in the evening. They did not speak, and Agnès was painfully aware of Alan's proximity, the tall man by her side who did his best to curb his big strides so she could keep up with him. He was at least two heads taller than she and walked with that American swagger Agnès so admired in him and his countrymen, as if they still needed to secure their supremacy over the Wild West.

Not knowing what to say but dying to ask questions, she decided to remain quiet as well, telling herself to just enjoy the opportunity of being with him. When they reached the boulevard that ran along the Seine with busy traffic going both ways – taxis, private automobiles, army vehicles, ambulances – Alan turned to her.

"Which way?"

"I live two miles to the left, near the Pont de Puteaux. Would you like to go in that direction for a bit?"

"You live near the Bois de Boulogne?" He sounded surprised, then added with an endearing chuckle, "ah, that's right, you're a Baroness. Had quite forgotten that. Gosh, you Europeans! Truly never met so much old blood before in my life. Every other person I speak to is a Viscount or an Earl of something."

Agnès bit her tongue but decided not to tell him she was not a Baroness by birth but had been adopted. "Would you like to walk along the waterside?" she suggested.

"Sure."

They descended the stone steps and went along the broad pavement, with boats and smaller barges gliding past in the diffuse afternoon light. The green spur of the Île de la Jatte was to their right. Agnès breathed in deeply. She liked taking this route home, close to the river, after a long day in the operation room. There was a fresh breeze in every season here, and the pungent scent of the water, cool as a mountain stream, always livened her senses. The dark water rippled in miniature waves, sloshing against the quay when larger boats passed. Green patches of vegetation drifted by, and silver-finned fish skittered under the surface.

They still walked in silence, each wrapped in their own thoughts. Agnès took regular, precise steps, her arms by her sides, her medical bag clutched in her right hand, while Alan, who walked hatless with his brown locks pushed away from his forehead, had his hands folded at his back.

Just when Agnès wondered if she should break the silence because it was becoming awkward, he said evenly, "Listen, Agnès, I had it all worked out. You've trained under me long enough to lead the team at the Lycée.

That was my reason for waiting to go up north – to make sure you'd be ready."

She was baffled by his words, but her heart swelled with pride at this promotion. "Thank you. I honestly didn't know you had so much confidence in me."

"I trained you, remember?" Again, that chuckle she had never heard in the operation room. It made him sound younger, more boyish.

"True." She gave him a shy smile, her eyes catching the last of the evening light.

"So, it would be rather inconvenient if you also decided to leave for the front."

"Doctor Davies could take charge."

Alan seemed to ponder this for a moment. "He might."

"It's not a whim, Alan. I've been considering this ever since the war started." And she told him of the sad circumstances of Château de Saint-Aubin.

He listened attentively but shook his head. "I'm not your father, just your mentor and supervisor, but if I *were* your father, I would simply forbid it." The stern professorial tone was back.

Agnès sighed. "I'm sure my father will be in total agreement with you. But what about the rumors that the Germans are considering a new offensive on the Western Front, now that Russia is no longer in the war? They could take Paris overnight, and I wouldn't be safe here either then."

"Then you could flee south, like everyone else will."

"As long as this wicked war goes on, nobody is safe anywhere," Agnès remarked bitterly.

"But there's a difference between seeking danger and staying relatively safe."

"The same goes for you."

Agnès wondered how it was possible she was talking in this manner to her professor, but somehow their walking together in civilian clothes with the bustle of her own city all around them made her ignore the distance they had always carefully observed. And she could not bear the thought of never working with him again. She was not done learning from him; she wanted more, more than this. So she decided to try one more thing.

"We're almost there. Would you care to come and meet my father, to see how he thinks about this ludicrous plan of mine?" She made it sound as light-hearted as she could.

Alan glanced at his pocket watch and then looked at the sky where the clouds were thickening. "I think I ought to be..."

"Please, Alan."

He glanced at her begging face then shrugged his shoulders in a comical way. "Oh, all right, then. I suppose I owe you something after all this time working together. If you want to fight two men, be my guest. Show us what you're worth." He grinned at her, and for a moment she felt incredibly close to him.

They left the pathway along the Seine at the Pont de Puteaux, and after crossing the Boulevard de la Seine, Agnès directed them to a stately mansion on the waterfront. The dark-green front door read in decorative golden lettering *Baron Maximilien de Saint-Aubin et famille.*

As soon as she opened the door with her latchkey, the housekeeper Madame Petit appeared from the front parlor looking questioningly at Agnès. "You're all right, Miss Agnès? You're very late!"

"Sure, Petipat, everything's fine. This is Professor Bell. Is Papa home?"

The ample-bosomed housekeeper nodded, straightening her massive black dress, and looked, slightly bewildered, from the young girl to the tall American who was standing rather stiffly on the doormat.

"Yes, yes, of course. Do come in, Professor Bell. Welcome." Busying herself with making room for them in the parlor, puffing up cushions and rearranging chairs, she addressed the young Baroness but secretly eyed Alan, giving Agnès inward glee at the effort the elderly woman was making at understanding what was going on.

"The Baron is in his music room, as usual," the housekeeper went on. "He was waiting for you, as he'll be going out tonight. Will you be going out as well, Miss Agnès?"

"No, Petipat, it's been a long day. Afternoon shift tomorrow, but still early bed for me." She glanced up at Alan, wondering what would happen tomorrow. He had not told her if he was leaving straight away.

"Now, I'll go and fetch your father, my girl." Moving as fast as her voluminous body allowed her, the housekeeper proposed before she disappeared in the hallway, "Do make yourselves at home, dears, and tell me what I can get you."

"Would you care for a sherry, Alan? Or maybe something stronger? My father wisely stocked his cellars before the war. We may run out of potatoes, but we've still got plenty of liquor." She giggled.

"A sherry will be fine, Ma'am," Alan said politely, but

as soon as the housekeeper had left, he lifted a quizzical eyebrow. "Petipat?"

"Oh, do sit down." Agnès laughed. "It's just my special name for her. She's been like a mother to me."

"Ah, I see. So, your own mother...?" Agnès nodded and hoped Alan would not probe any further in this sensitive matter, but after a while the silence hung heavily in the room, so she added timidly, "My mother died shortly after giving birth to me. I was raised by my father and Madame Petit, who has been with our family since the beginning of time."

"So sorry to hear that." Alan's brow softened with empathy. "If it's any comfort to you, I also lost my mother, though I have some vague memories of her as I was four at the time. My father remarried soon after, but I've never liked my stepmother, whom I was supposed to call Mother as well, and...well ...it's also influenced the relationship with my father." He stared wistfully at the blunt knives on the wall.

Agnès' kind heart went out to him immediately. "My time to be sorry. At least I've had a doting dad, and of course Petipat who's picked me up more times than I can remember."

The air lifted, and she followed Alan's eyes as they took in the room. She wondered what he would make of it and how different it certainly must be from his American house back home, with the parents to whom he did not feel close.

As all the rooms in the De Saint-Aubin household, this one displayed a mishmash of styles, ranging from conservative classic to quirky exotic, very much like the owner himself. The downstairs parlor mostly held

objects from the Baron's many trips to the African conti-
nent, so it was generally referred to as 'The African
room'; other rooms being labeled 'The West Indies
Room' and 'The Aboriginal Room.'

The majority of the furniture consisted of high-
backed Louis Quinze chairs and canopies in cream
chintz, but the coffee table was a wooden elephant
carrying a glass plate on its back, and there were a
number of rackety stools, carved antelopes, and naked
ebony statues, reminiscent of his expeditions into dark
Africa. The floor was carpeted with Persian rugs, but here
and there the skin of a lion or a tiger had been thrown on
top of them, trophies from his safari trips. Oval ancestor
portraits were juxtaposed with spears, knives, and other
primitive weaponry. It was chaotic, personal, liberal.
Agnès feared it gave her guest quite a glimpse into her
unusual background.

In a room upstairs, a violin abruptly stopped playing,
and a little later, voices could be heard coming closer.
Alan rose to his feet, thereby hitting his head against one
of the low-hanging candelabras.

"You're okay?"

He nodded, rubbing the crown of his head. "Damn
height. Never seem to get used to it." At that moment, the
Baron entered, with Madame Petit on his heels, followed
by a maid carrying a tray with glasses and a carafe filled
with amber-colored sherry.

Her father, although of modest height, at least
compared to Alan, managed – as always – to immediately
fill the room with his presence. It was not that Baron
Maximilien de Saint-Aubin was a remarkably handsome
man, nor very imposing, but there was a quality in his

posture, a mixture of what Alan had called 'old blood' and a personal artistic freedom, that made certain no one overlooked him. It was in the way he moved, elastic like a cat yet aristocratic in his uprightness, the elegant movements of his arms derived from a life-long practice as a musician, and the ease with which he carried himself, confident but never completely in tune with protocol and decorum. He had the creaseless olive-colored skin from his Spanish mother and the silver-streaked hair and honey-brown eyes of his late father, the 6th Baron de Saint-Aubin.

His clothing was always of good quality and often had a colorful, eccentric twist. Today he was wearing embroidered Persian *babouches*, simple charcoal flannel trousers with a clear fold in them, and a dark-blue pullover under which the collar of his white chemise, with the invariably colorful silk cravat tucked in.

A broad smile spread over his mustached face as he approached them, and it was typical of the Baron that he first went over to his daughter to plant a kiss on her fair forehead and compliment her on her loveliness before turning on his heels and greeting their guest. Agnès knew why he did this – to make clear that any man who might be interested in her would have to deal with the father first, but it embarrassed her as it was rude to Alan, who after all was her professor. And since she was twenty-three, there was really no reason for him to treat her as a little girl.

"Ahh, Professor Bell! Agnès has told me so much about you. Glad to finally make your acquaintance." He shook Alan's hand cordially and then seated himself in one of the Louis Quinze armchairs, putting one knee over the other and rearranging the flannel crease so it went straight over his knee.

Alan sat back down on the coach. Agnès noticed an uncertainty in him she had not seen before, and she inwardly cursed her father. He made a habit of making other people feel smaller than needed. While the maid handed round glasses, she decided she would come to the point straightaway, so Alan did not need to stay in her house any longer than he probably wanted.

"Papa, Alan... uh... Professor Bell is here for a reason, as you might have guessed." Her father took a contemplative sip from his glass and set it down on the side table before looking up at her.

Download In Picardy's Fields

ABOUT THE AUTHOR

Hannah Byron's crib stood near the Seine in Paris, but she was raised in the south of Holland by Anglo-Dutch parents. In her bestselling WW2 historical fiction series, *The Resistance Girl Series*, Hannah's heroines also traipse from one European country to the next, very much like their creator.

Now a retired university lecturer and translator, the European traveler and avid researcher still regularly crosses borders to learn about new vistas.

What started as curiosity about her family's connection to D-Day, evolved into an out-of-controlish study into WW2 history. To blame, or thank, must be Uncle Tom Naylor. If he'd not landed on the beaches of Normandy and helped liberate Holland, her British mother would never have met her Dutch Dad after the war.

Strong women are at the core of Byron's clean and wholesome romance novels. Every book is a tribute to the generation that started the women's lib movement, got dirty in overalls, flew planes, and did intelligence work. Today's girl bosses can but stand on the shoulders of these amazons.

Side-by-side with their male counterparts, Byron's heroines fight for freedom, equality and... love.

~

Under the pen name Hannah Ivory she writes Historical Mysteries. *The Mrs Imogene Lynch Series* stars the kind but opinionated Victorian widow of Constable Thaddeus Lynch.

ALSO BY HANNAH BYRON
HISTORICAL FICTION

The Resistance Girl Series

In Picardy's Fields

The Diamond Courier

The Parisian Spy

The Norwegian Assassin

The Highland Raven

The Crystal Butterfly

The London Spymaker (Preorder)

Box Set The Resistance Girl Series 1-4 (only ebook)

The Resistance Girls Revisited (preorder)

The Agnès Duet (spin-off):

Miss Agnès

Doctor Agnès

HANNAH IVORY

VICTORIAN MYSTERIES

The Mrs Imogene Lynch Series

The Unsolved Case of the Secret Christmas Baby

The Peculiar Vanishing Act of Mr Ralph Herriot

The Perilous Pursuit for Mr Banerjee's Gemstone (coming soon)

Printed in Great Britain
by Amazon